Mich

When A

Goes Bad

Michael "OoDoo" Smith

This book is a work of fiction. Names, characters, places, and incidents are the product of the author's imagination or used fictitiously. Any resemblance to actual events, locales, or persons, living or dead, is coincidental.

Author: Michael OoDoo" Smith
Editor: Teairo Preston
Cover Design: Tiffany Lee
Cover Model: @iam_infinitytherealest

ISBN-13: 978-0578417219

DEDICATION

This book is dedicated to my OG Carrie "Poon" Garth...I love you Grandma and I'm thankful for everything you taught me about life..

ACKNOWLEDGMENTS

All praises goes to Jesus Christ my Lord and Savior. I'm so very Blessed for GOD placing me in a situation where I was forced to find myself. Thank you Father for everything you've done and everything that you're gonna do for not only me, but for all of your children.

Rest in Peace Josephine "Miss Tootsie" Bolden-Smith my Great Grandmother who installed the belief of Jesus Christ not only into her entire family, but also into anyone who crossed her path along her journey on the earth until she departed us to go to her home in Heaven...

To my mother's Carrie, Kathleen, Roberta and Erica I am so blessed to have loving mothers like ya'll...Uncle Rickey, what it do...My sisters Teairo and Tiuna, ya'll already know big bruh love ya'll til death My brothers Darnell & Da'rell, Gory & Gregory, I am my brothas keeper. CJ and Justice, unc love ya'll.

Tiffany Lee thanks for working with me, which I know gets hard at times. To my seven angels Bud, Aniya, R.I.P Kayden, Makari, Karmyn, Logan and Lenoxx, just know that ya'll daddy loves ya'll with all of his heart. Much love to the Smith and Bolden Family .Big Cousin John Reedus, Big E, Brownie, Black Baby, Blake, Jeremy B.. Dae Dae...The Candy Clique....And anyone I forgot I'll get you in the next novel. This just the beginning...

Shout out to the entire cities of Decatur and Huntsville, AL...My whole Stonegate Family Northwood. Sunset..."BT ".. Northside, Southside, Northwest, Southwest, East Acres and Lincoln Projects. All the strip clubs, Bardershops and Beauty Salons.. Special thanks to anybody who has something negative to say about me or my literary works...It's you who keep me grounded on making

my craft reach the streets.. Thanks for all your motivation..
To my HATERS, GOD bless ya'll!! Last but not least anyone who jumped ship on me like a pirate, I appreciate you showing your true colors....Yours Truly,

" OoDoo "

When A Good Girl Goes Bad

CHAPTER 1

"Girl, I'm so nervous! I ain't never did no shit like this before." Kira had butterflies in her stomach as she prepared to dance in the strip club for the first time of her life.

"Bitch, you gone be straight. Plus it ain't even nobody out there like it was when Candy started last week. At least this gonna be both of our first time." Niece tried to calm Kira's nerves with a small pep talk.

JaKira Brown, TaNiece Johnson and Candice Watts had become best friends a year ago when they started college as freshman at Alabama A&M in Huntsville, Alabama A.K.A. The Rocket City A.K.A Hunts Vegas. Huntsville got its names because it's one of the most happening cities in Alabama. Kira was from Birmingham, Alabama, TaNiece was from Nashville, Tennessee and Candice was from Charleston, South Carolina where her mom is a dope fiend. Her grandmother was the only person looking out for Candice, but she got killed in a church shooting. Candice's father had a 25-year sentence in the Feds for crooked cops and a drug conspiracy. Kira and Niece's families had a little money to support them with, but Candice was all on her own. Candice was more about her business than the other two girls.

The girls had been having money problems and had become tired of eating Ramen Noodles. Even more so they were tired of being victims of the broke ass college dudes, who only wanted to sneak into their dorms, smoke a blunt with them and the try to fuck. Last week Kira and Niece rode to the Players Club with Candice. They had no idea that Candice was gonna participate in the Amateur Night at the club, but she did, and she made the quickest and easiest five hundred dollars that she had ever thought about making in three hours.

"Okay bitch! Let's go to the bar so I can get a drink to relax, shit." Kira said as she looked at her 34-27-45 frame in the mirror. Standing five foot seven inches, light brown skin with jet black hair that went past her shoulders. Kira was a star. Most people compared her to Maliah Michel. The white negligee she had on made the other girls in the dressing room look at her with hate in their eyes.

"That's my bitch! Come on let's turn up." Niece adjusted her size 36C breast inside the push up bra she was wearing as her and Kira exited out of the dressing room. Niece stood 5'8" and she was a cheeseburger away from being considered fat, but she had no stomach. With her mocha chocolate skin, real gray eyes and an ass like a donkey. Niece knew she was killing shit as she ran her fingers through her silky finger length hair. She had pretty, full lips that made people say she looked like Candy from the group Xscape.

"Got damn! New booty on duty," DJ Yella Boy screamed over the music as he gawked at Niece and Kira, fantasizing about gettin in between either one of their legs. It didn't make him a bit of difference about which one it was either.

****

Drop had been out all night serving fiends, trapping off of his phone. That's how he got the name Drop from serving crackheads the best shit. It was said that his crack was so good that it would make you drop dead if you couldn't get any. So, of course Drops trap phone rang non-stop every day and night. Tonight, he was tired of driving, so he figured he would stop by the Player's Club since he was down the street. He hadn't been in there in over a year because the last time he went to the Player's Club he damn near caught a stray bullet. So, until tonight he had taken the Player's Club off of his to-do list.

Wearing a pair of Jordan gym shorts, a wife beater and a pair of Jordan flip flops, Drop knew he could get inside the club with no smoke from security since he knew the manager Big Tony. Drop got searched by security then he walked to the bar where he ordered a shot of Patron, a Corona with lime, and three hundred singles. The local strippers knew who Drop was and they all spoke to him. His five eleven, chocolate and muscular, one hundred and ninety pound frame, which was accommodated by his wavy hair and bottom gold grill made him attractive to most women. Drop walked to the back of the club and took a seat in a chair against the wall. He took a sip of his beer then he sat the bottle down. When Drop looked up at the stage his eyes got stuck on this young tender who was foreign to him. He watched her as she playfully danced with the girl beside her.

"Girl, that nigga over there is fine as hell, and he won't stop looking at you." Niece screamed in Kira's ear over the music while she pointed in Drop's direction. When Kira looked in the direction Niece was pointing her eyes locked with Drop's eyes. Drop mouthed the words "come here" with a head nod signal. Kira got off the stage and went and sat beside Drop.

"What's up lil baby?" Drop leaned in closer to Kira so she could hear him over Gucci Mane's "Rain Man" blasting from the speakers.

"Nothing! What's up with you?" This was Kira's first conversation with someone in her new field of work and she was sort of nervous.

"My name Drop! Are you new here? I've never seen you here." Drop could tell Kira was a few years younger than him.

"I'm Kira and yes this is the first time I've ever danced."

"So, you telling me this is your first night ever dancing?"

"Yeah, me and my friend Niece." Kira pointed to Niece.

"Have you made any money?"

"No." Kira started giggling.

"So, is Kira your real name?"

"Yes, it is."

"Lil Baby, you gotta have a stage name. So, what is it gonna be?"

"I don't know." Kira shrugged her shoulders.

"Magic." Drop said smiling exposing his dimples.

"I like that." Kira agreed with her stage name.

"Me too! I like the magic in your eyes."

Even though Drop didn't know Kira he held concern for her in his heart. Drop knew it didn't take much for a young woman to get caught up in the lifestyle of the strip club and lose focus of their dreams and goals in life. Drop decided to find out what Kira's story was. She told him she was a sophomore at A&M and her major was Design & Fashion. Drop could tell that Kira came from a good family and she had a head on her shoulders, but she needed a little guidance. They conversated for almost an hour. They siped on Patron Margaritas, something that Drop knew Kira could handle. He didn't want her to get drunk because somebody might try to take advantage of her.

Drop hipped Kira about things she didn't know about the strip club. He warned her about situations and the bullshit that comes along with stripping in a club. Kira could tell that Drop was known in the city because damn near all the people who either worked in the club or came in the club to party knew who Drop was and spoke to him. Kira was so hypnotized by Drop that she had forgotten about the reason she had come to the club, to work. Drop had her in a trance.

Niece was on the stage on her knees and elbows with her ass in the air, shaking it for two dudes that were throwing a few dollars at her and the girl next to her. Niece looked at Kira, who was laughing and having fun talking to Drop. That bitch ain't made one dollar with her dumb ass, thought Niece as she slapped her ass, a move she seen one of the other strippers do. The next thing she knew the guys behind her started slapping dollars on her ass.

"The more you show them is the more money they'll spend boo." Sweets a thick brown skinned stripper with tattoos all over her body told Niece, while she shook her ass next to her. Niece didn't have to be told twice. She pulled her bikini string to the side and exposed her pussy and ass hole to the dudes that were tipping her. The dudes started throwing more money.

"Follow my lead boo!" Sweets told Niece and Niece nodded her head okay. Sweets rolled over onto her back and pulled Niece on top of her. Sweets could tell that Niece was tense.

"Just keep shaking that ass baby. They like it when two girls do this." Sweets was under Niece humping her and slapping her ass at the same time. The dudes started making it rain on Sweets and Niece. Niece started smiling when she saw all the dollars raining on them.

"Change positions boo!" Sweets coached Niece, but what Niece didn't know is that Sweets was getting turned on from the girl on girl action.

Money on the floor,
Lighters on tha dresser
Drop my top,
No one could do it better
Diamonds in tha leather,
Wood and chrome
Boppin ass bitches just won't leave me alone.

Big K.R.I.T., Eightball, MJG and 2 Chainz blasted from the speakers.

"I thought you said it was your friend's first night" Drop pointed at Niece who was butt naked on the stage humping Sweets from the back, slapping her on the ass. What the fuck, thought Kira as she watched one of the dudes that was tipping Niece touch her pussy. Drop watched Kira's facial expression and he could tell that she wasn't the least bit interested in letting a nigga stick his finger in her pussy for a dollar.

"Magic, Magic! Drop called Kira's stripper name twice, but she didn't answer. "Kira!" Kira turned to Drop when she heard her name. Drop couldn't help but to laugh. "Look lil baby, this might not be for you. Here, take this!" Drop handed Kira the singles he got when he first came in the club.

"What's this for?" Kira was confused. She hadn't danced for Drop and he gave her three hundred ones.

"Put my number in your phone." Kira pulled her phone out of her money bag and punched in Drop's number. "Call me if you need me and remember what I told you." Drop downed the rest of his drink then he got up and left the club.

As soon as Drop left out the club, Kira went and got dressed. She wasn't sure if she could dance at the club. One thing was for sure though, Niece had gotten completely comfortable with her new gig.

"Where you bout to go? I seen you over there with that fine ass nigga." Candy asked Kira when she walked in the dressing room and saw Kira in her regular clothes.

"I'm bout to go to the dorm. I'm having second thoughts

about this shit." Kira frowned up her face.

"Only the strong survive, Kira. You think about it before you jump in the water with the sharks." Candy told Kira. Then Kira left out the dressing room and told Niece she was about to leave. Niece told her to go ahead, she would find a way home.

Kira woke up at 7:30 a.m. to get ready for her nine o'clock class and she seen that Niece wasn't there. Maybe she stayed with Candy, thought Kira as she called Niece's phone only to not get an answer. Next Kira called Candy.

"Hello," Candy answered as she pulled in the drive through of McDonald's on North Memorial Parkway.

"Hey girl, have you talked to Niece?"

"You ain't gonna believe what I'm bout to tell you bitch, hold on. Let me get a number one with a large orange juice."

"Aye, bitch order me a meal too." Kira was hungry.

"Make that two number ones with orange juice, but yeah bitch when you left the club last night Niece and the girl Sweets was acting like they was eating each others pussy. Niece let Sweets rub on her pussy. Them hoes put on a lil miniature freak show for them niggas." Kira's mouth fell to the floor while she listened to Candy.

"Hell nah, girl! Tell me you're lying."

"Can I get some grape jelly? No bitch I ain't lying and you know I gots it recorded on my phone. Bitch I'm on my way to the dorm." Candy hung up as she pulled off from McDonald's.

When Candy made it to Kira's room they ate breakfast while they watched the freak show Niece and Sweets put on in the club.

Kira and Candy were disgusted with Niece's actions. They were about to leave out of Kira's room to go to class when Niece came through the door with Sweets. They smelt like ten gallons of liquor and a weed plant.

"Ya'll hoes missed out last night. You know them niggas gave ah bitch a band to dance for them when the club closed." Kira and Candy looked at each other while Niece bragged.

"Yo ass must not be going to class?" Kira asked Niece.

"Hell naw bitch! I haven't even been to sleep, plus I'm bout to move out of this dorm and move in with Sweets." Kira and Candy couldn't believe Niece, but they had no choice but to believe her when they seen her start packing her belongings.

"Are you sure you wanna do that?" Kira was concerned about Niece but she could tell that Niece had her mind made up. Sweets looked at Kira with a look that said "Bitch try again", and smirked.

"Hell yeah Bitch! Sweets get that laptop for me."

"Come on Kira, let's go to class." Candy grabbed Kira's arm and led her out the door.

"Fuck that bitch! That's her life and if she wanna throw it away then go ahead and let her." Candy told Kira as they walked down the hall. Kira knew Niece was fucking up bad, but there was nothing she could do about it, so she went on to class.

While Kira sat in class, she couldn't help but to think about Drop and all the things he told her about the lifestyle that comes with dancing in the club. Kira couldn't believe how she was watching his words come to life so fast through Niece. When class was over Kira called Drop, but he didn't answer, so she went to the school library and filled out some job applications online.

Drop heard his phone while it rang, but he was too busy whipping and flippin in the kitchen to answer the number that he didn't know. He had to get finished with the order he was cookin to serve a coupla niggas that was comin from Decatur. Drops wrist game was amazing. He could turn a brick of cocaine into almost two bricks of cooked crack. A lot of guys shopped with Drop because of his cheap price and good quality.

Schruur Schruur Schruur

Was all you could hear while Drop was in the kitchen standing over the sink at his grandma Cal Mae house. Carl Lee, Drops' father walked into the kitchen wearing a creased down bootleg Polo outfit with two fake gold rings on his fingers. To be a crack smoker, he was cleana then ah muthafucka. He walked over next to where Drop was standing and broke a small chunk of crack off of one of the cookies that drop had cooked.

"Mane what the fuck you doin?" Drop couldn't stand when somebody invaded his space while he whipped and flipped.

"Got damn mane, I'm just bout to test this shit out for ya! Shit bout ain't no good no got damn way!" Carl Lee picked with Drop knowing that he couldn't stand fa somebody to be in the kitchen with him.

"Mane, get that shit and get back till I get done, mane damn!" Carl Lee left out of the kitchen and went to his room which was the basement of his mama Cal Mae's' house. Cal Mae had purchased the house before Drop was born and Carl Lee was git. She used to hustle back in her day but now the only thing you can get from seventy year old Cal Mae was a dollar shot of bottom shelf liquor, and a hot out the grease fish sandwich. And if she didn't know you, you better not knock on ha doe.

Drops' mama and daddy were dope fiends or like they call them in the Rocket City, "Bubs." Sonya, Drops' mama was at Tutwiler Women's Prison in Alabama, where she'd been for the past three years for trafficking cocaine. Drop had gotten her a lawyer who got her Color Code, but Sonya wouldn't stop getting high. To keep his mama off the streets turning tricks for crack, Drop always gave his mama something to smoke. Cal Mae told Drop, "Boy when God gets ready for yo mama and daddy to stop smokin dat shit, he'll make they ass stop." Drop believed his grandma.

By the time Drop finished cooking and sacking up everything, Carl Lee came back into the kitchen shining a flashlight, but it wasn't dark. Drop knew he was high because he had the flashlight on and his mouth was twisted. Drop couldn't help but to laugh even though it hurt him to see his daddy like that. He laughed to keep from crying. That's normally how shit went with Drop, he took the bitter with the sweet.

"That's it right there ain't it?" Drop watched Carl Lee peek out of the kitchen blinds.

"Yeah, yeah, yeah, the, that, that's it right there." Good crack often gave Carl Lee a speech impediment.

"Give me your keys so I can go catch this play." Carl Lee got the keys to his 96 Chevy Lumina out of his pocket and gave them to Drop. Drop threw Carl Lee the keys to his 72 pearl white convertible Chevy Caprice, that sat on 32 inch forged Ashanti's. The entire inside of the car was red Ostrich skin. Drop never worried about Carl Lee fucking up his car because even though Carl Lee was a smoker, he was still a real street nigga.

"I'll hit you up later." Drop grabbed his pack and left the house to go handle his business.

CHAPTER 2

"Ahh, yes baby yes!" Niece cooed as she gyrated her hips while her high school boyfriend Jared ate her pussy. He had never ate her pusy like this before. It was like he knew all the right places to lick. Niece spread her legs wider.

"Yesss, baby right there!" Niece reached down to rub on Jared's head and when she did, she felt long silky weave.

Niece woke up from the wet dream she was having to find Sweets sucking on her pussy. What tha fuck, thought Niece's mind but her body was screaming for more and more. She was confused about if she should make Sweets stop or not, but right then Sweets went even harder on her and began rubbing on Niece's wet ass hole while She ate her pussy, causing Niece's hormones to over power her will power.

"Squip, squip, squip!" Sweets looked into Niece's eyes while she sucked on her clit. Then Sweets penetrated Niece's ass hole with the tip of her index finger. "Ahh, oohh fuck!" Niece screamed as she felt pleasure that she had never felt before. Ha. I got this lil bitch now, thought Sweets as she completely stopped what she was doing and stood up from the sofa. Niece didn't want her to stop.

"Come on baby, let's go to the bedroom" Sweets smiled seductively at Niece who had a spaced out look on her face. Sweets grabbed Niece's hand and led her to the bedroom. As soon as they made it inside the bedroom Sweets stripped out of the t-shirt and boyshorts she had on. Niece did the same. Sweets laid on the bed on her back. "Come here baby." When Niece climbed into the bed Sweets directed her into a sixty-nine position putting Niece's ass on her face.

"Siii, ooh." Moaned Niece when Sweets spread her ass cheeks and stuck her tongue inside of her pussy. Niece began riding sweets face while Sweets fucked her pussy with her tongue. "Oohh, ooh yess." Niece screamed when she felt Sweet's thumb go inside her ass. Niece had to bite her lip from the pleasure she was feeling.

Sweets raised Niece off of her face then sat up. Next she pushed Niece onto her back on the bed. She gotta know she about to eat this pussy, thought Sweets as she positioned Niece. Oh my god, I've never ate a woman before, thought Niece, but it was too late because all she could feel was Sweets dripping wet pussy cover her lips. Niece tried to move her face away, but she couldn't because Sweets was grindin her face hard.

"You better eat that pussy." Sweets told Niece then she leaned down and started sucking Niece's clit while she rode her face. "Hmmm, hmmm," moaned Niece then she stuck her tongue into Sweets creamy pussy. Sweets couldn't help but smile as she felt Niece's tongue slide in and out of her pussy. Sweets started bouncin her fat ass on Nieces face like it was a dick.

"Ahh, shiit! Eat that pussy boo!" Sweets stopped bouncing on Niece's face then she took her three middle fingers and started rubbing on Niece's clit real fast from side to side.

"Ohh, ahh, ooh, shit Sweets. I, I'm bout to cumm." Niece's body began to jerk as she climaxed. Satisfied with her job, Sweets stood up from off of Niece and watched the after affects of Niece's orgasm. I got her lil ass hooked now, thought Sweets as she climbed off of the bed.

"Bay, we gotta be at work in a few hours. I'm about to shower." Sweets leaned down and stuck her tongue into Niece's mouth. They kissed passionately for a minute before Sweets raised up and walked to the bathroom. Niece was in another world as she layed in the bed naked with a wet pussy. She couldn't believe how good Sweets had made her feel.

****

Kira sat on her couch wondering why Drop hadn't called her back while she watched a rerun of Love and Hip Hop in Atlanta. She was about to call and order a pizza when her phone rang. It was Jeremy Burgess A.K.A. JB, the star of the A&M basketball team. Kira felt her heart flutter when she saw his name on her caller ID. She'd had a crush on JB since she first laid eyes on him a year ago in their Black History class. They had a few small conversations in class and exchanged numbers, but that was as far as it went. Now out of the blue JB was calling her phone.

"Hello." Kira answered in her sexy tone of voice.

"What's up shorty?"

"Nothin! What's up with you?"

"Trying to see if you was going to work tonight." A lump formed in Kira's throat that made it hard for her to swallow. How does he know that I dance, thought Kira.

"I don't know what you talking about JB, work where?" Kira tried to play stupid.

"Come on ma, my partna Duke say he slid through the Playa's Club and saw you in there working last night. JB lied. Actually, he had rode by Kira's dorm this morning and stopped to holler at Niece when he seen her packing her stuff into Sweet's car. When he asked Niece what she was doing, she told him that her, Kira and Candy worked at the Playa's club and that they were all moving off of campus because they were making plenty of money. Then she upped her roll of money on JB. JB figured since he had gotten kicked off the basketball team for failing a drug test for cocaine and his family cut him off financially for being stupid and rebellious, that he needed to get himself a chick that was bringing in some money like what Niece showed him. He waited till he thought the time was right and he called Kira.

"Oh, I was there for amateur night. I really didn't dance like that." For some reason Kira felt embarrassed.

"Aww, well I guess I won't be going there tonight since you won't be there." JB was running reverse psychology on Kira. Damn he was gonna come see me, thought Kira.

"I'm in my dorm if you wanna come chill." Kira couldn't let

the opportunity to chill with the pretty light skinned JB who stood 6 foot 4 inches, with real green eyes, natural curly hair and both of his arms were sleeved with tattoos. Kira knew JB could have any girl on campus so she was gonna consider herself lucky and try to get the dick from him tonight.

"I guess I can come by there for a second. What room is it?" JB didn't sound too enthused about chilling with Kira, but that was part of his game plan

"Room 202B." Kira said happily.

"Bet!" JB hung up

Kira jumped from the couch and ran to the shower. She couldn't wait for JB to come over. She had heard about how he be slangin wood on the chicks he be fuckin. They all be Dickmatized by him. Twenty-five minutes later JB knocked on Kira's door. Kira jumped up from the couch, ran to the door, looked through the peephole and there he was. She quickly opened the door.

"What's up?" JB grinned.

"Hey, come in!" Kira turned around and started slanging her ass from side to side as she walked back to the couch. JB shut the door then he saw how Kira's ass was jiggling in them AAMU gym shorts she had on. Yeah, I'm gonna fuck the shit out of this lil hoe, thought JB as he gripped his dick through his pants while he walked to the couch. When he sat down he pulled out a blunt of gas from his pocket.

"Can I smoke in here?"

"Not really, but I guess!" Kira knew the campus police be

walking the dorm halls, but she was willing to chance it for JB. While JB lit up the blunt, she stuffed a wet towel under the bottom of the door to prevent the weed smoke from drifting into the hallway.

They sat in total silence while they smoked and watched videos on MTV Jams. They looked at one another occasionally. As soon as the blunt went out, JB looked between Kira's thighs and saw how fat her pussy was sitting. He wanted to press the gas on her and fuck, but he was on a mission. He put his sad face on and stared at the TV for minutes without looking Kira's direction. Kira looked at JB and she could tell something was bothering him. He's not acting like hisself, thought Kira knowing that JB was normally full of life. After several minutes of silence Kira broke the ice.

"What's wrong with you? You're not acting like yourself." JB turned to Kira and stared deeply into her eyes. She was immediately hypnotized by his eyes.

"I got kicked off the team for fighting. My family disowning me. I don't have money for food, gas, or anything else. I don't know what I'm gonna do. My parents wont even let me move back home." JB made his situation sound worse than it was. His parents had actually begged him to move back home.

"Damn, I'm sorry to hear that!" Kira hated to see JB looking so down. She wished there was something she could do to help him.

"I know right! It's cool though, fuck it! My phone gets cut off at twelve tonight if I don't pay the bill. That shit two hundred dollars. I don't know how I'm gonna pay it, but fuck all that baby, what's up with you?" JB leaned over and laid his head on Kira's breast as if he needed somewhere to rest his problems.

"Nothing for real! I got a couple of dollars if you want it JB." JB smiled on the inside when he heard Kira's offer. She bit the bait, thought JB.

"I can't take your money baby. You don't even have a job." His plan was in motion. JB moved his hand onto Kira's thick thighs and began rubbing on them. Kira felt a warmness sweep over her whole body. A tingling sensation mingled between her thighs. When she felt JB's hand move upward toward her juice box, she opened her legs enough for him to slide his fingers between the shorts she had on. When JB touched Kira's pussy it was soaking wet and his dick jumped rock hard when Kira's wetness drenched his fingers. JB lifted his head from Kira's breast and met her lips with his. While they tongue kissed, JB used his free hand to lift Kira's shirt up over her breast. Once her shirt was up, he stopped kissing Kira and put her left breast into his mouth while he penetrated her pussy with two fingers.

"Hmmm, hmmm." Kira began breathing heavy from the action but she needed more so she pulled her shorts down for JB to pull them off and he did. Then he stood up and got completely naked while Kira did the same. When she saw how long and thick JB's dick was, she saw why the girls go crazy about him.

"You have a condom, don't you?" Kira wasn't trying to catch any STD's or get pregnant.

"Damn, I knew I forgot something!" JB put his boxers back on and sat down next to a disappointed Kira. JB laid his head on her breast.

"I guess it wasn't meant to be." Said JB as he started rubbing on Kira's thighs, getting her hot all over again. Kira couldn't fight temptation and she gave in.

"Don't nut in me JB!" Her words made JB smile. He hated using condoms. He hadn't wore a condom since he'd been at school at A&M.

"I ain't baby, come here." JB sat up straight and pulled Kira on top of him. Then he pulled his dick out of his boxers.

"Ooh JB!" Kira felt the head of JB's thick eight inch dick go inside of her. She began riding JB and he put his hands on both of her ass cheeks.

"Ahh, yess, ahh." Kira screamed as she jumped up and down on the full length of JB's dick. She had pussy juice running down JB's balls. Her pussy was super soakin wet and the best that JB had ever had, but he couldn't let Kira know that. Only problem was he couldn't hold back the nut that was creeping to the head of his dick.

"Ahh ahh ooh." Yelled Kira, feeling like she was about to cum, but JB raised her off of his dick.

""Ah shitt" moaned JB as he nutted on his leg. Kira was disappointed that she didn't get her nut, but she had to admit that JB was everything that she had heard he was. Kira got up and went to the bathroom to get JB a wet rag, but by the time she made it back to him he already had on all of his clothes. Damn, he doesn't even wanna wipe himself off, thought Kira as she watched JB adjust his clothes.

"I don't mean to rush off, but I gotta find out how I'm gonna pay my phone bill by midnight." JB was sticking to his game.

"Hold on!" Kira went to her purse, pulled out ten twenty dollar bills and handed them to JB. Even though he was happy, JB kept his game face on.

"Baby, I don't know if I'll be able to pay you back."

"Don't worry about it. I think I'ma see if they'll let me work at the club tonight. Kira had a plan to make her money back.

"Thanks baby, and if you go to work call me and I'll swing through to see you." That made Kira smile.

"You'll come see me for real?"

"Yes baby."

"Okay. I'll call you."

JB gave Kira a big hug, a kiss and slapped her on the ass then he left her dorm. That shit is going to be easier than I thought, JB thought to himself as he walked to his car. When he crunk up his car, the time on the radio read 8:15 p.m. Fuck, I gotta hurry up and catch the mall before they close so I can cop the new J's, thought JB as he pulled off.

Kira couldn't believe that she had fucked JB, the most popular nigga in the school. She felt like she had accomplished something. She couldn't wait to tell Candy and Niece. Kira showered, got dressed and then she called Candy to tell her the news.

"Hello!"

"Bitch, you ain't gonna believe who just left this pussy." Said Kira when Candy answered the phone.

"Whoever he was I hope he ain't broke and you made him pay for it." Kira felt odd by Candy's words.

"JB girl!" Kira screamed like she hit the lotto.

"Ha! Kira, dude broke and he got kicked off the team for snorting powder. He ain't shit to get excited over." Candy gave it to Kira straight up and raw. She didn't give a fuck if she killed Kira's vibe. Kira felt like Candy was just hating that she fucked JB and she hadn't.

"Are you goin to work at the club tonight?" Kira changed the subject.

"Yeah bitch, that's how I'm gonna stack my money. I'ma be there every night. I ain't got no mama like you and Niece. I can't be on no lil girl shit." Candy's tone was serious.

"Okay, damn, my bad! Come pick me up before you go." Kira didn't mean to rub Candy the wrong way.

"Alright!" That girl so damn naive, thought Candy as she hung up the phone.

****

"Is that all I can get for you Drop?" Que, the sales lady at Footlocker in the Madison Square Mall asked Drop, as she walked behind the register to ring up the shell toe Adidas that Drop was about to buy. Drop seen that they had released a new pair of Jordans that morning so he decided to get them for his nephew Bud Bud.

"Do you got a size four in these?" Drop held up the shoe.

"Let me go see." Que walked to the back of the store switching her fat ass in the tight uniform she had on.

"Aye Que! Let me gone and ring up my partner while you look for those shoes!" Eric yelled to the back where Que went to. Eric went to AAMU also.

"Go ahead!" She yelled back. Drop moved to the side to let the dude get rung up.

"I didn't think your ass was gonna make it up here to get them," said Eric.

"Man you know I didn't have all the money, but I fucked Kira and she gave me two hundred dollars." JB bragged. Drop couldn't help but to hear their conversation because he was right beside them. There's a thousand girls named Kira, thought Drop as he shook the idea of JB and Eric were talking about the girl he'd met at the Player's Club last night.

"Damn, she tippin like that. I heard that her, Niece and Candy worked at the Players Club now! That'll be $225 player." JB handed Eric the money. Nah that's not her thought Drop.

"Shit, you might wanna ride to the Player's Club with me tonight to see if you can snag one of them lil hoes that work there." JB told Eric.

"Bet! Hit my phone up before you go." Replied Eric.

"Aight!" JB grabbed his shoe bag and left the store.

"Aye lil homie, you go to A&M?" Drop asked Eric.

"Yeah, it's my second year." Drop had all the confirmation he needed. Dumb ass lil hoe gonna give anotha nigga the money I gave her. No flex zone, thought Drop as he pulled out his phone and called Carl Lee. He told Carl Lee to pull his new black Suburban that sat on thirty-four inch Larenzo's out of the storage in the back of Cal Mae's house.

Drop left the mall and went to his condo in Montesano Terrace and took a shower. He knew everyone in the club would have on urban gear so he wanted to separate himself by dressing casual. He put on a pair of Gucci Khakis with a short sleeved red and green Gucci Polo shirt with brown leather Gucci loafers on his feet. Drop looked at himself in the mirror as he sprayed himself with Aqua Di Gio by Gorgio Armani and he couldn't be more pleased with himself. The five karat studs he had in his ears made the waves in his temp fade appear to be deeper. After he sprayed himself with cologne, he threw on his plain jane gold Rolex watch and his gold Gucci link chain that weighed 1008 grams on his neck. Seconds later Drop left out his front door with a few bands in his pockets to party with. It had been over a year since he flexed in the club.

When Drop pulled up at Cal Mae's house to get in his truck, he couldn't help but to smile and laugh when he saw Carl Lee posing beside his truck while his white girlfriend Shelly took a picture of him. If you didn't know any better when you looked at Carl Lee's Facebook page, you would think that he was a Super Trapper.

"Whoo, got damn! Baby you sharper than a broke dick dog! Aye bitch take a picture of me and my baby." Carl Lee put his arm around Drop's neck and they took a pic.

"You can keep the drop tonight, I'm out." Drop jumped into his truck and inhaled the smell of the new leather interior.

"Call me if you need me baby, and be careful. Aye and if you see your sista tell her I said brang me my grandchild." Carl Lee yelled to Drop as he reversed out the driveway.

"Aye baby, gone down to my room and wait for me to get back. I'm about to bust me a block in the drop." Carl Lee told Shelly.

"Baby why can't I go with you?" Shelly wanted to know.

"Cause bitch, you do as I say do! Now take yo funky ass down there and wait on me to get back. It's a lil something for you on the nightstand." Carl Lee jumped into the convertible.

"I swear I get tired of these bitches talkin. If it wasn't for dem bitches suckin the skin off ah nigga dick I swear they wouldn't need no mouf." Carl Lee said out loud as he pulled off from the house.

Bwou Bwou Bwou Bwou

Was all that could be heard when Drop pulled into the parking lot of the Player's Club. Drop had that dumb ass slap in the back of his Suburban. He had eight 13.5 JL Audio Woofers and each Woofer was running off a 2500 JL Audio amp. When the music in his Suburban was on low it sounded like King Kong was fighting Godzilla in the back of the truck. Drop parked near the entrance of the club. This was his first time driving his truck so nobody knew who he was. The girls parked next to Drop was boppin extra hard trying to get Drop's attention. He smiled at them then jumped out the truck lookin like a million bucks and walked into the club. He was about to pay the doorman, but Big Tony the club manager called his name and waved him over. Drop walked over to him.

"What's up, OG?" Drop dapped Big Toney.

"Shit! Koolin baby boy! They told me you fell through here last night."

"Yeah, I stopped through and had a drink, but tonight I need that turn up in my life. I know you got something for me." Drop was ready to go to Molly World.

"You know I gots you nephew!" Big Toney raised up the napkin that was under his hand and Drop grabbed the eightball of Molly that was under it.

"What I owe you?"

"That's on me baby. Hell I ain seen yo ass in ah year." Big Toney was glad to see Drop. He didn't vibe with many young cats but he fucked wit Drop the long way. Whenever Drop couldn't get work from his normal plug, he would shop with Big Toney.

"I had to lay back and run that check up, unc! Aye baby let me get ah bottle of Patron and a thousand singles." Drop told the bartender while he talked to Big Toney. When the bartender gave Drop his order he tipped her fifty dollars.

"I'm bout to go to the back and get right Unc!"

"Okay, I'll be back there to holla atcha in a few!"

Drop left the bar with his bottle in one hand and his singles under his arm. When the lights hit his ice the diamonds twinkled and glistened. Drop was lit up like a Christmas tree. He found a table in the corner and posted up. He scanned the club then he poured some Molly into his mouth and washed it down with Patron. Future's song "Super Trapper" blasted from the speakers as Drop started slightly rockin his head. Every nigga in the club felt like their shine had been stolen by Drop and every bitch in the club wanted to be with Drop. When he looked across the room he saw Kira sitting in the lap of the same dude who was talking bout her at Footlocker, Drop smirked. Strippers walked up to Drop one by one speaking and asking to give him a dance, but he declined, gave them a few dollars and then sent them on their way.

Candy walked out of the dressing room and the first thing she saw was Drop shining like new diamonds. Then she looked to her left and saw Kira hugged up under JB. She about one dumb ass hoe, thought Candy. Candy couldn't believe how stupid Kira was. JB only trying to use her and she didn't even know it. Candy had to put her friend up on game before she let a money machine walk away for a nigga who ain't got cheeseburger money. Candy walked over to Kira and pulled her by the arm.

"Come here bitch!" Candy yelled over the music and Kira got up to see what she wanted.

"What's up girl?" Kira closed the dressing room door.

"Yo dumb ass out there hugged up wit JB broke ass when dude who blessed you down last night standing over there by hisself shining like lightning." Candy had her hand on her hip.

"Girl, I ain't stuttin dude. Me and JB about to be a couple." Kira was stuck on stupid and Candy saw it. Candy walked out of the dressing room. She couldn't stand to listen to another word from Kira's mouth. Candy walked to the stage where she rested her elbows and started shaking her ass. She watched Kira go sit back in

JB's lap. The sweet smell of a man's cologne filled Candy's nostrils. There was somebody behind her tipping her but she didn't know who it was. Candy turned around to see who it was and she saw it was Drop showering her with money. Drop smiled at Candy and she smiled back before she turned back around. Got damn he too damn fine, thought Candy, as she shook her ass in circles. Thirty seconds later the song ended and Drop went and sat down at his table. Candy picked her money up off of the floor and stage then she walked over to Drop.

"Thank you handsome for the love you showed me." Candy knew that Drop had tipped her three hundred easily.

"You welcome, beautiful," replied Drop, then he took a swig from his bottle of Patron. Candy knew from the intro that Drop wasn't anything like the dudes she went to school with even though he didn't look much older. She knew he was a hustler by the vibe that he gave off. That hoe might be stupid, but I'm not, thought Candy.

"I'm gonna go to the back and freshen up. Is it okay if I come back and chill with you?" Candy wanted to get acquainted with Drop.

"Fo sho lil mama! I'll be right here!" Drop told her.

Candy looked at Kira as she walked to the dressing room. Kira was laughing with JB and his friend. Candy couldn't do nothing but shake her head. While she freshened up, Candy couldn't help but to think about her heroin addicted mother. Her mother's addiction is what motivated her to go hard in the paint. Unlike Niece and Kira's families, Candy's family didn't have money. Candy quickly shook off the thoughts of her mother and left out the dressing room to join Drop. As soon as she sat down beside Drop one of his favorite R&B songs came on. "Wicked Games" by the Weekend came blasting through the speakers.

"I left my girl at home, I don't love her no more."

Drop stood up and started singing along with The Weekend. The Molly had kicked in and Drop was feeling righteous. He started throwing money on himself while he sang and jumped to the music. Candy sat smiling as she watched Drop. She was feeling Drop and she didn't even know his name yet. When the song went off Drop sat down.

"You like that song, don't you?" Candy could tell that Drop was feeling hisself.

"Yeah, that's that shit! What's your name sexy?" Drop liked what he saw when he looked at Candy. Her skin was paper sack brown and her cheeks had dimples. Candy's eyes were hypnotizing hazel brown. Her body was bangin. Slim waist, thick thighs and a real nice round booty. She kept her nails manicured and her feet pedicured. Not to mention Drop loved the bob hairstyle that Candy was rocking.

"Candy, but my real name is Candice." Drop liked her introduction.

"Well, I'm Drop, but you and only you can call me Ivan." While Drop and Candy got acquainted, Niece and Sweets walked up to where they were sitting and started picking up the money that

Drop had thrown.

"Get yall thirsty asses back! That's her money!" Drop flexed on Sweets and Niece.

"Ain't shit about me thirsty, my boy!" Sweets got loud with Drop.

"Bitch you thirsty if I say you thirsty." Drop put his finger close to Sweets face, Candy jumped up from her seat and got in between the two of them, because it looked like they were about to get into a physical altercation. Drop reached over Candy and grabbed the top of Sweet's head pulling her to him. When they hugged Niece and Candy looked at each other like, what the fuck is going on. After they hugged, Drop went in his pockets and brought out two hundred dollars. Sweet already knew that the money was for Bud Bud's daycare.

"I bought Bud Bud some shoes today and Carl Lee said bring him his damn grandchild ASAP." Drop told his sister.

"Okay and give me some of that shit you on. I see you biting on your lip." Sweets knew Drop was high on the Molly.

"What you think about her?" Drop pointed to Candy while he got the Molly out of his pockets to give to Sweets.

"She straight! Hell she ain't been working here but a week and she don't conversate with nobody but the girls she goes to school with." Candy listened to Sweets give her a good report to Drop. Drop looked at Candy and nodded his head yes, while he smiled.

"You can gone bout ya business now I need to holla at your

soon to be new sister." Drop told Sweets

"Okay then!" Said Sweets and she walked away with Niece trailing behind her.

"I thought yall were about to fight!" Candy told Drop when they sat down.

"Nah, that's my sister."

Drop and Candy got to know one another for a good hour before Drop got ready to leave. Before he left they exchanged numbers and agreed on a set date for a date, two days later.

"That chain that nigga got on ain't real, and that ain't real Gucci he got on." Said JB hating the fact that Drop was flexin.

"I know right my nig. That's probably Gucci lil cuzin Lucci that he wearing." Said Eric and they burst into laughter.

"That hoe Candy wish she had a nigga like me, but I'm with you baby." JB hugged Kira.

"So you mines now?" Kira wanted a label.

"Yeah baby, but is you gonna keep working to make us some money?" JB wanted to know what she was gonna do before he put a label on it.

"Yeah baby, I'm gonna make sure we straight!" Kira told him. JB smiled. Mission complete, thought JB.

"Okay! Then we together. I'm about to get up out of here so you can make daddy some money." JB gave Kira a hug and a kiss then left.

When JB and Eric walked out of the club, they saw drop getting inside his Suburban, then he started it up. The music that pounded inside the truck felt like an earthquake.

"Got damn! That bitch pounding and she supa clean!" Eric gave Drop his props.

"Man that shit alright, but it ain't all that." JB was hating as he unlocked the door on his Camaro that his parents was paying the car note on.

"I bet if I put this 380 in that nigga face he'd come up off of everything." JB grabbed his pistol from under the seat and cocked it. He had so much hate in his heart. He hated to see another man with what he wanted. He didn't even know Drop, but he hated him.

CHAPTER 3

It seemed like Kira was stripping just to support JB's habits. Everytime she turned around he needed money for something. Kira had saved a thousand dollars for the first full week she worked at the club. She was saving the money to move into an apartment, but before she could get the rest of the money she needed, JB told her he needed the money to get his car fixed. Kira later found out that he used the money to buy some cocaine to use. She cried but she got over it. Two weeks after they started dating JB's parents repossessed his car without telling him. He came outside of his dorm and saw his car being towed away on a tow truck. The students in the parking lot were laughing at him. JB was embarrassed as hell. That left him with no other choice, but to drive Kira's Camry while she was at work or school, where she was rarely going to class.

"Jeremy, don't be late picking me up!" Kira reminded JB before she got out the car to go into the club. He had already been late 3 out of 4 days that week.

"Bitch, ain't nobody gonna be late. Get the fuck out of the car." JB got loud with Kira when he saw Sweets and Niece walking past the car. Kira knew better than to say anything back. He had already slapped her two nights ago when she asked him who the girl was calling his phone.

"Ain't no way in hell that nigga would be talking to me like that. I would've been had my brother off his ass." Sweets told Niece as they walked into the club.

As soon as Kira got out of the car JB turned the music sky high and smashed out the parking lot. He had people to see and places to be. He sped down Governor's Drive to the Parkway and went north to go pick up his snorting partner, Lil Tim who was at his girlfriend's house on Grizzard Road. JB pulled into the driveway of the house where Lil Tim was approximately ten minutes after he dropped Kira off. He blew the horn. Lil Tim came outside and jumped in the car.

"What's up, my boy?" Lil Tim was ready to get geeked.

"Not shit! What's up witcha?" JB reversed out of the driveway.

"Shid, my boy, I know where that fish scale at! Lil Tim knew where the best cocaine in town was at.

"Make the call then nigga. I got half on a quarter!" JB had built up a high tolerance for cocaine real fast. He sniffed at least an eightball a day by himself.

"Say no more, my boy!" Lil Tim unlocked his phone and made the call.

"What's up my boy? Bay, get me some sour patch kids and a red icee." Drop and Candy were about to see the new movie by Ice

Cube. "This Friday."

"What's good big bruh?"

"Shit. what it do?"

"Not shit! Need me a quarter of soft."

"You know where the Monaco Theater at, don't ya!"

"Yeah."

"Call me when you get outside."

Since the night they met at the club, Drop and Candy had been spending a lot of time together. They were really feeling each other. This date at the movies made their 20th date in a month's time. Drop had a surprise for Candy tonight. He was gonna wait right before the movie started to give it to her. Earlier in the day Drop had stopped by Kay Jewelers and bought Candy a five karat diamond ring that he paid seven thousand dollars for. It was a relationship ring. Drop was ready to make Candy his girl and he was about to do it tonight. Candy was the only girl he had ever talked to longer than a week without attempting to hit the pussy.

Drop and Candy walked to their VIP section seats after they got their zoom zoom and wham whams. The waitress came and they ordered drinks. When the waitress came back with their drinks, Drop was about to make a toast to their relationship and give Candy the ring, but his phone rang. Damn, thought drop realizing how fast he'd forgotten that he'd told Lil Tim to come to the theater. Normally, Drop wouldn't even do no shit like serve no nigga while he was on a date, but Lil Tim was like family and he wanted exactly what Drop had in his car. Drop answered his phone.

"Aye, park by Bar Louie's! I'm bout to walk out." Drop told Lil Tim.

"Alright ! Aye bruh, park over there." Lil Tim instructed JB who had just snorted an one and one.

"I'll be right back bay! Let me catch this play." Drop leaned over and kissed Candy on her lips. Candy was really feeling Drop but she didn't know how he really felt about her, therefore, she held onto a skeleton in her closet.

"Hurry up because the movie is about to start!" She reminded Drop.

"Okay bay!" Drop got up from his seat and sped walked to his car so he could get the quarter ounce of cocaine to give to Lil Tim.

"Give me your money, there goes bruh right there." Lil Tim told JB when he saw Drop coming out of the theater. JB looked and seen that it was only one person walking in their direction of the parking lot and it was Drop, the nigga he hated for some unknown reason. Oh shit, it's that bitch ass nigga Candy talk to, thought JB, hiding his excitement about what he was about to do. JB handed Lil Tim his half of the money for the cocaine. Lil Tim got out of the car and walked up to Drop's classic 96 Impala which was all factory except for the smoke tint on the windows. Drop saw Lil Tim walking up to his car as he opened the door and got in. Drop leaned over and got the quarter of cocaine out of the glove box.

"What's up my boy?" Drop spoke to Lil Tim, who was standing between Drop and the open car door so nobody could see what they were doing.

"Shit, big bruh! Just koolin! I was_____" was all Lil Tim got to say before he was pushed from behind by JB who had a bandana tied around his face.

"Nigga take everything out of your pockets and throw it on the ground." JB yelled while he pointed his gun at Drop who was still sitting in the driver seat of the car.

"JB, what the fuck is you doin?" Without thinking, JB pointed the gun at Lil Tim and shot. As soon as he shot Lil Tim, Drop rushed him and the gun went off again. Drop fell on top of JB.

"Aiii, they're shooting!!" Screamed pedestrians who were now running through the parking lot.

"Errrr!" JB used all of his strength to push Drop off the top of him, and he stood up seeing that Drop's blood was all over him.

"Agghh shit!" Drop moaned from the burning pain. JB rolled Drop onto his back then went in Drop's pockets taking all of his money. JB snatched Drop's Jesus peace necklace from around his neck then he grabbed the cocaine from off the ground and ran back to his car. JB sped out of the parking lot. What the fuck were you thinking! Mane fuck that shit. I'm straight! Shit! Shit! Shit! JB thought to himself as he drove in the direction of the Player's Club to go pick Kira back up.

"Agghh fuck!" Drop grunted in pain. He looked to his left and saw Lil Tim on the ground bleeding.

What's taking him so long, thought Candy, as the previews ended. She picked up her phone and called Drop's phone. When she didn't get an answer a gut feeling kicked in and she left out of the movies to go see if she saw Drop. As she walked closer to the car, she saw a crowd of people hovered over something. Then she heard an ambulance siren approaching.

"Hold on buddy! Help is on the way!" Candy heard one of the people say, as she approached the crowd.

"Oh my God! No!" Candy screamed as she fell to her knees by Drop's side when she saw him on the ground bleeding.

"Baby please don't die." Cried Candy, burying her face in Drop's shoulder.

"Bay!" Drop had lost a lot of blood and was feeling weak, but he mustered up the strength to call Candy, Bay. Candy raised her head from his shoulder and looked into his eyes.

"Yes baby? I'm here and help is on the way. Baby just stay with me." Drop tried to gain strength to talk.

"Reach in my back pocket." Candy hurried and reached in Drop's back pocket, thinking there might be some drugs inside of it. When Drop saw Candy pull out the ring box he smiled.

"I love you!" Drop closed his eyes.

"I love you too baby! Wake up, baby, please wake up!" Candy cried.

"Everyone move back. Ma'am you're gonna have to move away from the victim." The EMS people told Candy. They loaded Drop into one ambulance and Lil Tim in another.

Candy couldn't ride in the ambulance cause she wasn't family so she followed the ambulance in Drop's car. Candy sat in the hallway of the emergency room waiting to talk to a doctor. She pulled the ring box out of her pocket and opened it. Oh my God! It's gorgeous, thought Candy as she stared at the most beautiful diamond ring that she had ever seen. Her emotions became unbalanced and she started crying. Candy closed her eyes and began praying. "Dear lord, I know I don't serve you like I should, but I'm coming to you asking you to please bring Ivan through this situation, God please. I beg of thee." Before Candy could say Amen she felt someone touch her on the shoulder. Candy opened her eyes and it was the doctor.

"Ma'am, aren't you here for Ivan Sweets?" The doctor asked Candy with a smile on his face.

"Yes sir! Is he okay?" Candy asked nervously but she knew God was on her side.

"Yes ma'am. He's gonna be absolutely fine. The bullet didn't hit any major arteries or organs. We removed the bullet. He's getting stitched up right now. He'll be moved to a room to rest in a few minutes." Candy couldn't smile any bigger as she jumped up and hugged the doctor.

"Thanks Doc!" Candy released her embrace.

"The nurse will let you know what room he'll be in, in about fifteen minutes." The doctor patted Candy on her shoulder then he walked off. As soon as the doctor walked off, Sweets, Cal Mae and Carl Lee came bursting through the door of the emergency room waiting area.

"Where my baby at?" Cal Mae hollered at the nurse sitting at the reception desk.

"Candy!" Sweets ran over to Candy who was smiling when Sweets spotted her. Sweets knew everything was fine by Candy's facial expression.

"He's fine! The bullet has been removed and they have stitched him up. I'm just waiting on them to tell me what room he's gonna be in." Candy informed Sweets.

"Grandma, he okay!" Sweets yelled at Cal Mae who was giving the nurse at the reception desk G-shit.

"Got damn it, he betta or I'ma kill me some muthafuckas!"

"Mama, calm down fo they put us out dis hospital. This pretty lady is just doing her job." Carl Lee shot the nurse a flirtatious smile. Candy filled them in on what little bit she knew while they waited to be told what room Drop was gonna be in.

****

Kira grinded on the customer's lap with her top off exposing her pretty breasts. It was her first dance of the night. She looked to her left and saw JB walking in her direction. When he got close enough he snatched Kira by her arm.

"Bitch, go get dressed. We gotta go!" JB barked at Kira, who didn't have a clue to what was goin on.

"Aghh, Jeremy! I can't just leave my job!" Pleaded Kira.

"Aye bitch, I've paid you for this dance already!" Said the upset customer standing to his feet. JB pulled out his pistol from under his shirt and hit the dude across the head, knocking him out cold.

"Now come the fuck on, Kira!" JB started pushing her towards the entrance to the club.

"I gotta get my purse and clothes."

"Bitch, you better get that shit and be at the car in two minutes. Don't make me come back in this club." JB tucked away his pistol and ran out of the club.

Kira went to the dressing room to get her belongings and Big Toney came in right behind her.

"Magic, you can't work here anymore lil baby. Your lil crackhead ass boyfriend gone make somebody kill his ass. I know yo folks girl. You deserve better than that." Big Toney chewed on a toothpick the whole time he talked to Kira. He was from Birmingham so he knew some of Kira's people and he knew she didn't have to be doing any of the shit she was doing. All Kira could do was cry as she got dressed. She grabbed her stuff and ran out of the dressing room. What that bitch got going on, thought Niece when she saw Kira run out of the club. Soon as Kira got into the car JB sped away from the club and headed in the direction of the campus. Kira sat in silence as he drove while she looked at the blood that was all over his shirt and pants.

"Come on, we gotta pack your shit fast, we movin!" JB parked in front of Kira's dorm. Kira was confused as to what was going on but she knew better than to question JB.

They went inside and started packing all of Kira's belongings. Technically, she packed while JB snorted cocaine and counted the money he robbed Drop for. JB counted thirty eight hundred dollars and stuffed the money into his pockets. Then he got up and started taking Kira's bags into the car.

Oh my God! Kira thought when she saw the diamond flooded Jesus necklace laying on her couch. JB had dropped the chain when he pulled the money out of his pocket. Kira knew that it was Drop's chain because she had seen him with it on in the club. Kira became scared for her life. This explains why Sweets ran out of the club as soon as we made it to work, thought Kira. She quickly grabbed the necklace off the couch and stuffed it into the side pocket of her luggage, where she figured JB wouldn't look at. As soon as she zipped up the bag JB appeared in front of her. Kira's heart stopped beating. She just knew she was caught.

"Come on, bitch. We gotta go." JB snatched the bag from off the floor and took it to the car. Kira exhaled from relief of JB not knowing she had Drop's necklace. When she got into the car, JB drove down South Parkway to the King's Inn Hotel, where he paid for a room for a week.

****

"Boy, I'm sholl glad you okay cause yo grandma was about to pull a John Q in this muthafucka!" Carl Lee had everybody laughing as they sat around Drop's bed.

Knock Knock Knock

The door to Drop's room came open and two detectives came in.

"We're sorry to intrude in on you at such a critical time, but we need to ask you a few questions Mr. Sweets, if you don't mind."

Said the bald headed black detective wearing some tight ass slacks. For some reason, Candy got nervous when the detectives came into the room. She hated cops. Her father was serving twenty-five years in the Feds behind some dirty cops.

"Okay! Ask!" Drop said sarcastically.

"Could we talk alone?" Said the skinny pale white detective.

"Nah, whatever you got to ask me, you can ask me in front of my people." Drop sat up in the bed.

"Well, do you know who your attacker was?" Said the white detective.

"No sir, I don't." Drop replied.

"Do you know a Timothy Wiggins?" Said the black detective.

"No sir, I don't." Drop knew that was Lil Tim's real name. The detectives looked at each other and they knew they were wasting their time. They had just questioned Lil Tim before they came to Drop's room and he denied knowing anything about the shooting also. The white detective pulled out his card and handed it to Drop.

"If you hear or find out something, give us a call." Drop took the card.

"I'll make sure I do that!" Yeah right, thought Drop. He was glad Lil Tim had stuck to the code by not saying shit. The detectives left the room no closer to finding out anything than they were before they came to the hospital. Drop balled the card up and threw it at the trash can.

"Well brother, I'm glad you okay, but a bitch gotta go get her money. I know Candy gonna take good care of you as many rocks that ring has that you got her." Sweets had a smirk on her face because she knew Candy's little secret.

"Yo brother in the hospital and all you can think about is making yo booty clap, girl, get out this room fo I put my foot in that big ol ass of yours." Cal Mae had everybody laughing.

"Aghh!" Drop moaned from the pain of laughing.

"Baby, don't laugh so hard." Candy laid Drop's head back.

"Hell, come on Carl Lee. Dat girl gone take care of that knucklehead. I left my chitterlings cookin. We gotta go fo we ain't got nowhere to live. You know chitterling juice can cause a grease fire." Cal Mae had everybody laughing again. Carl Lee walked over to Drop and kissed him on the forehead.

I'll be back to check on you later on baby. He told Drop.

****

"Spend ah check and get it right back" Dae Dae blasted from the speakers while Niece grinded on the lap of Fat Rabbit, a local trap nigga that was making a name for hisself. Fat Rabbit had been coming to the club on the regular for the past month and he had a thang for Niece. He knew she fucked with Sweets but he still wanted her. Fat Rabbit caressed Niece's body while he tipped her at the same time.

"Baby, you know a nigga want you." Fat Rabbit spoke into Niece's ear. She couldn't deny the fact that she was feeling him too. She looked forward to seeing Fat Rabbit come into the club. He always made her laugh and he only tipped her whenever he was in the club. That spelled loyalty to Niece but she was naive.

"So you really want me daddy?" Niece figured she could show Fat Rabbit a lil love tonight since Sweets was gone to check on her brother.

"You know I do baby!" Replied Fat Rabbit. Niece looked around to make sure that nobody was looking and she unzipped Fat Rabbit's pants. She stuck her hand inside and found his already hard dick. I see why they call him Fat Rabbit, thought Niece when she grabbed a hold to his short, fat dick and pulled it out of his pants. Fat Rabbit shifted in his seat to get more comfortable.

"You like that?" Niece whispered in his ear while she stroked his dick.

"Hell yeah baby!" Fat Rabbit threw more dollars on Niece while he enjoyed the hand job he was receiving. He wanted to feel the inside of Niece so bad that he tried to sit her on top of his dick, but Niece locked down on his lap cause she knew what he was trying to do. What Fat Rabbit didn't know was that Niece wanted to feel him inside of her just as bad as he wanted it. She was fiending for some real dick. It had been over a month since she felt a man inside of her.

"Do you have a condom?" Fat Rabbit damn near nutted right then from the excitement of just knowing he was about to get inside of Niece.

"Yeah baby. I got one." Fat Rabbit fumbled around in his pockets, found the condom then handed it to Niece. Niece put the condom on for Fat Rabbit and the she sat on his dick and started gyrating her hips, acting as if she was just giving him a lap dance.

"Ahh, oohh Rabbit!" Niece moaned from the pleasure of Fat Rabbit's dick stretching her pussy walls.

Sweets walked past the bar heading to the dressing room to get dressed. When she got near the back of the club, she saw Niece in the corner straddled on Fat Rabbit's lap, but there was something about the way she was riding him. Sweets was about shake off the thought of Niece fuckin Fat Rabbit, but then she saw Fat Rabbit start pumping Niece from the bottom. Awe, this bitch got me totally fucked up, thought Sweets but she managed to keep her composure and walked to the dressing room. Sweets feelings were sort of hurt. It's not like she wasn't a woman, but she knew the game. That's why she only fucked wit women because she could control her feelings more and not go head over heels for them like she would a man. Sweets hadn't been with a man since she had her son. Her baby daddy done her so wrong that he drove her to the point where she damn near hated niggas. I'm gonna show the lil bitch how it feels to get played with, thought Sweets with a smirk on her face as she got dressed. Niece walked in the dressing room and damn near jumped out of her skin when she saw Sweets standing right in front of her.

"What you all jumpy and shit fa?" Sweets laughed on the inside knowing that Niece was just as guilty as she wanted to be.

"Awe, um, cause I thought you was gone to check on Drop." Niece was nervous as hell. To top it off, she had the condom that Fat Rabbit used balled up in her hand.

"Yeah, I just left the hospital! He good, but you wouldn't

know since you ain't called to see. But anyway, I'm bout to try to make me some money." Sweets walked out of the dressing room. Fuck that was close, Niece thought, as she went and sat on the toilet and dropped the condom between her legs while she took a piss.

Sweets walked to the bar and ordered a shot of Patron. She licked the back of her hand and poured some salt on it. Then she turned up her shot, next she licked the salt off the back of her hand. When Fat Rabbit came out of the men's restroom, Sweets was the first person he saw and he walked straight up to her at the bar. Normally Sweets wouldn't have given Fat Rabbit the time of day but tonight she was about to drain him for every dollar that she could.

"Damn, you look good enough to eat!" Fat Rabbit licked his lips. Tonight might be your lucky night, thought Sweets, then she....

Clap Clap Clap

Sweets made her ass clap three times

"Nigga you can't afford this!" Sweets knew how to make a nigga spend that check on her. First you belittle his pockets, then you twist up your lips and walk away from them. As soon as Sweets walked off from the bar, Fat Rabbit waived the waitress over and ordered a thousand singles.

By the time Niece came out the dressing room from washing up and changing, Sweets had Fat Rabbit pouring money on her while she danced on the stage. Sweets saw Niece's facial expression change for the worse when she saw what was going on. This is just the beginning boo. I'm gonna hit you where it hurts later, thought Sweets, as she pulled her lace thong to the side letting Fat Rabbit get a glimpse of her pretty freshly shaved pussy. Niece felt stupid for what she had done cause now Fat Rabbit's full attention was on Sweets. He had never tipped Niece like he was tipping Sweets. Before the night was out, Sweets had gotten Fat Rabbit to tip her fifteen hundred and he hadn't smelled the pussy.

****

From the moment that JB and Kira checked into their hotel room, JB paced back and forth to the window peeking out of the blinds. Kira took a shower then laid in the bed and started scrolling on facebook where she saw where Candy made a post thanking God for blessing her man through his situation. When Kira saw the post, she figured Drop was okay. Thank God, thought Kira, then she sat her phone down and looked at JB who was breaking cocaine down on the nightstand. She watched JB scoop some cocaine up with a key and sniff it. JB raised his head and caught Kira staring at him.

"Fuck you lookin at?" Growled JB. Kira rolled her eyes and picked up the remote to the tv, but that was the wrong thing to do. JB became enraged. He walked over to Kira and grabbed her by her hair.

"Ow! JB, let me go!" Kira kicked and screamed while JB dragged her off the bed onto the floor to the table he had the cocaine on.

SMACK!

"Bitch, you lookin at me like you better than me or something!" JB said after he slapped Kira in the eye. Then JB pulled out his gun, cocked it and put it to Kira's head.

"No, Jeremy! Please don't shoot me!" Kira cried, fearing for her life.

"Bitch, scoop some of that shit up with that key and sniff it up your nose." Kira knew better than to do anything besides what JB had told her to do. Her hand shook from her nerves being rattled as she picked up the key and scooped some cocaine up. Tears fell from Kira's eyes like a waterfall and her stomach did backward flips as she brought the cocaine to her nose. Kira closed her eyes.

SNIFF

When Kira opened her eyes, the entire room was bright as the sun. She had a lump in her throat. Kira squinched her face and swallowed. JB lowered his gun from her head.

"Now look at yourself how you was lookin at me." JB smirked and began peeking out of the window again.

Kira touched her face but she couldn't feel it. I can't feel my face, thought Kira remembering how her face was hurting when JB first slapped her. She got up from her knees and went to the mirror. Her face was swollen on the left side and she had bags under her eyes. Kira's heart pace sped up and she had to go sit down on the bed. JB walked up to her holding out a beer.

"Drink this. It'll calm you down." Kira grabbed the beer and started drinking it. When she brought the bottle from her mouth, JB grabbed the bottle and sat it on the nightstand. Then he laid Kira on her back and began kissing her on the neck.

"You know I only act the way I act because I love you, baby!" JB said softly in Kira's ear as he slipped his fingers between Kira's shorts and touched her pussy. To her amazement, her pussy was wet and JB's touch felt like magic. JB took his hand out of her shorts and raised her shirt over her head. Then he stood up and got naked. JB stroked his limp dick, but it wouldn't get hard so he laid down and told Kira to give him some head.

SLURP SLURP SLURP

Kira sucked away at JB's limp dick for ten minutes but it still wouldn't get hard. Kira started getting agitated and the feeling in her face started to come back. She stopped suckin on JB and went to the night stand the cocaine was on.

"Sniff it up both nostrils." JB instructed Kira, and she did as she was told. Then she ran through the rest of the beer. A rush swept over her body and she no longer felt the pain in her face. She kneeled back down between JB's legs and went back to sucking and jerking on his dick. Kira was trying everything she knew to do to get JB's dick hard because she wanted to fuck, but she had no luck. After another five minutes of sucking and jerking she gave up.

"Baby, what's wrong? I'm so horny," Kira wanted to fuck.

"I'm high right now!" JB was mad his shit wouldn't get up.

"Can you give me some head then?" Kira said smiling, hoping that this would be her lucky night since JB had never ate her pussy. JB raised up with an attitude.

"Bitch, you know I don't get down like that, so don't try to play me." JB thought eating pussy was disgusting. He jumped up from the bed and put his clothes on.

"I'll be back!" JB grabbed the keys to the car and to the

room and then he left. Kira watched JB leave by looking through the blinds. As soon as her car was out of her sight, Kira jumped back into the bed and grabbed her phone. She uploaded X videos on google then she clicked on orgies and she began watching a video of Roxy Reynolds, Pinky and Montana Fishburne fucking each other with dildos and eating each other's pussy. Kira held her phone with one hand while she rubbed on her pussy with her other hand.

"Haaa, oohh!" Kira moaned as she found pleasure in watching the women fucking one another. She stuck two fingers inside of her wet pussy and then she took them out and stuck them in her mouth, tasting her own juices. After she sucked her savory juices off of her fingers, Kira began massaging her pussy.

"Ohhh, shit. Ahhh!" Kira rubbed on her swollen clit in fast circular motion.

"Emm, emm fuck!" Kira moaned. A midst of sweat formed on her forehead as she worked her pussy while she watched the porn. Just when she felt like she was about to cum, the room door swung open. JB caught Kira with her hand in the cookie jar and he started laughing.

"So you gotta wait til I leave to play with ya whack ass pussy." JB nodded his head. Kira just looked at him not seeing the problem.

"Kool, I might as well get wit me another bitch for the night. Maybe she can get my dick hard." JB grabbed his pistol which was the main reason he came back so fast. Then he left out of the room again.

"Jeremy!" Kira yelled after JB. She jumped out of the bed to try to catch him, but she was too late. When she opened the door he was pulling off.

All alone inside the room by herself, Kira sniffed cocaine, drank beer and played with her pussy all night long until she fainted, asleep at five o'clock in the morning.

****

Sonya looked at her reflection in the mirror while she brushed her teeth. Her bronze, caramel skin, hazel brown eyes and perfect set of white teeth made her beautiful. When she smiled, dimples implanted her cheeks. If you looked at Sonya, you would never guess that she was a recovering crack addict veteran of twenty-three years. She stood five feet six inches and had long, jet black hair that was braided to the back in cornrows. She weighed a healthy one hundred and fifty pounds making sure she watched her figure by exercising daily. At the age of forty-two, Sonya was still full of youth. Her size 34 C cup breast and 42 inch hips accommodated by a round firm ass made her extremely attractive in the eyes of men and women. When she finished brushing her teeth and washing her face, Sonya went to her bunk where she took off her sleep wear and put on her blue khaki prison uniform. Lay Lay, a young chocolate complexion female who looked like Kelly Rowland, handed Sonya a cup of coffee.

"Thanks bay!" Sonya gave Lay Lay a kiss on the lips. Sonya and nineteen year old Lay Lay had been in a relationship for the past four months.

"Baby, I hope you make parole today." Lay Lay hoped that

Sonya made parole today because she EOS her sentence in thirty days and she had fallen deep in love with Sonya.

Sonya took a liking to Lay Lay six months ago when Lay Lay had first come to Tutwiler Women's Prison in Alabama. When Lay Lay first got to the prison, a group of girls were hating on her because she was young and pretty. The girls tried to jump Lay Lay but Sonya saw what was goin' down and she wasn't having that. She made Lay Lay fight each girl head up. Even though Lay Lay didn't win every fight, she gave each girl more than they expected. Ever since that day Sonya and Lay Lay hung together. Sonya taught Lay lay the ropes of prison.

One day Sonya and Lay Lay were eating a burrito when out of the blue Lay Lay told Sonya that she wanted to taste her. Sonya was completely taken by surprise by Lay Lay's statement, but Sonya seen a look in Lay Lay's eyes that was full of honesty and lust at the same damn time. Later on that night, Sonya took a shower and when she came back to her rack there was a hump put up on her rack. Sonya shook her head smiling then she moved the cover to the humpback and climbed inside where she found Lay Lay wearing a prison-made negligee. Lay Lay had candles burning in the corners of the rack. She lit up a joint off of the candles. Sonya and Lay Lay got high then made sweet love.

"Yeah, baby. I hope I make parole too. That way I can be out there waiting for you to come home." Sonya lit up a cigarette to smoke with her coffee.

"So what are you gonna do when you get out?" Lay Lay

loved Sonya.

"I'm gonna stay away from the hood. I know that much. I'll most likely stay with my son for a minute until I get myself together.

"What will your kids think about me?" Lay Lay's words always reminded Sonya that Lay Lay really wanted to be with her.

"You know my son is gonna like you. I can't say that about my daughter cause I haven't talked to her." Lay Lay knew that Sonya and her daughter weren't on good terms with one another.

"Baby, go grab the hitta so I can call my son to see if he's gonna make it to the parole board this morning to speak on my behalf." Lay Lay went to their hiding spot and got their cell phone. She took the phone to Sonya. Sonya dialed Drop's number then stuck the phone inside a toboggan and laid back on her rack with the tabbogin to her ear, acting as she was just laying down while Lay Lay hot-railed to make sure the CO's weren't coming.

RING RING RING

Drop was knocked out asleep when his personal phone started ringing loudly. Candy picked his phone up and saw that it said "Mom" on the caller ID, so she decided to answer it since she knew Drop's mom was locked up.

"Hello." Candy answered the phone.

"Hey, who is this?" Sonya knew that Drop must be really feeling whoever this woman was answering his phone.

"This is Candy, Drop's girlfriend!"

"Oh, well this is his mother. Can I speak with him?"

"He's sleep. We're at the hospital. He got shot last night." Candy explained. Sonya felt her blood pressure rise.

"He okay, ain't he?" Sonya was now worried.

"Yes ma'am. He's fine. They removed the bullet and stitched him up last night. We just waiting for the doctor to release him."

"Damn!" Sonya said out loud without even knowing it.

"Ma'am, is everything okay?" Candy heard Sonya cuss.

"Yes baby. Everything is okay. I just thought he was gonna be at my parole hearing in Montgomery at ten o'clock this morning." Candy looked at the time on her phone and saw that it was ten after six. I could make it down there, thought Candy.

"I can assure you that somebody will be there on your behalf. I got you, Momma!" Candy put a smile on Sonya's face.

"Okay baby. Thank you so much! Tell Drop to call me when he wakes up."

"Yes ma'am. I will." They hung up. Sonya got up and handed the phone to Lay Lay to put up. Lay Lay saw Sonya had a worried expression on her face.

"What's wrong baby?" Lay Lay asked her.

"My son got shot last night. But he's okay." Sonya fired up a cigarette.

Candy got Carl Lee's phone number out of Drop's phone and called him. She told him to hurry up and come to the hospital to sit with Drop so she could go take a shower and get dressed so she could make it to Sony's parole hearing. At the mentioning of his baby mama's name, Carl Lee flew to the hospital to sit wit Drop. He wanted to see the nurse from last night anyway. Carl Lee was at the hospital fifteen minutes after he hung up the phone with Candy. As soon as he walked in the room Candy kissed Drop, told him she loved him and then she left to go get ready to leave.

****

"Rewind that part right there!" Detective Grubbs told Detective Collins as they watched the surveillance footage of the shooting that they got from Bridge Street Security.

"Stop right there. See Ivan coming out of the theater?" Said Grubbs.

"Yeah, and there goes Timothy getting out of the passenger side of that Camry." Said Collins.

"Yep, he's going to the same car Ivan just went and got inside." Grubbs told Collins as they watched the video.

"Yeah, Timothy's standing in the front of Ivan."

"Look! With the scarf around his face getting out of the driver's side of the Camry Timothy just got out of." Grubbs bit into a cream-filled pastry.

"Damn, he shot Timothy first. Then he shot Ivan."

"Snatched Ivan's chain from his neck and went in his pockets."

"We've got a robbery and two first-degree assaults."

"Nah, fuck'em. They didn't wanna help yesterday so I know this shit will never hold up in court." Grubbs knew that what they were looking at was nothing more than a drug deal gone bad.

"Yeah, you right! Pass me another donut!"

****

RING RING RING RING

"Cughh! Cughh! Cough!" The caller coughed while he listened to the phone ring.

"Alabama State Parole Office. This is Secretary Allison speaking." Said the woman.

"Yes. Could you transfer me to Parole Supervisor Daws if you don't mind. Cughh! Cughh! Cughh! Said the caller.

"Please hold sir." The woman transferred the call.

"Supervisor Daws speaking."

"How is your day?" The caller asked.

"It's fine. How can I help you?"

"I wanna make your day wonderful. There should be a package arriving to you from Federal Express. Make sure you make the instructions happen. Thank you!" The caller hung up. Daws was startled by the call.

KNOCK KNOCK

"Come in!" Yelled Daws

"I have a package for you from Fed Ex," Secretary Allison

handed Daws the shoe box size box and she left his office. Daws was sorta scared to open the box, but his curiosity got the best of him. When he opened the box, his day went from good to incredibly fantastic when he saw the stacks of money inside the box. A small piece of paper was on top of the money. Daws unfolded the note.

$200,000. Make sure that Sonya Mitchell makes parole today. Thanks Buddy!

Daws took a picture of the note with his brain and shredded the note. He typed Sonya's name into his computer and saw that her hearing was at ten o'clock. He looked at the clock and saw that it was nine o'clock. Daws picked up the phone and made the call he needed to make sure Sonya's parole was granted.

CHAPTER 4

Sweets slipped a Xanax in Niece's dark drink last night before she left the club. Therefore Niece was calling the hogs while Sweets got the money that they had put in the cookie jar and she took the money Niece had in her purse. Then Sweets threw some clothes and a few other items around the house to stage a break-in. Satisfied that the apartment looked like someone had broke in Sweets left. She drove to the nearest pay phone and called the police to report a break in at her apartment in Hillside Village off of Bonnell Drive. When Sweets got off the phone with the police, she went and got her son from the babysitter and went to the hospital to check on her brother.

Knock Knock Knock

"Is there anyone inside?!" The cop yelled who responded to the break-in call for Sweets apartment.

When nobody answered back, the cop stepped into the apartment since the front door was wide open. With his hand on his gun, he scanned the front area. He didn't see anyone, but he heard a noise coming from the back room. What is that? Thought the officer as he pulled his gun from its holster and walked to see a but naked woman in the bed sleep, snoring extremely loud. He looked around to see if there was anybody else in the apartment. Convinced that there was nobody else in the apartment, the cop shook the bed to wake the woman up.

"Ehmm! What bay?" Niece groaned without opening her eyes.

"Ma'am, ma'am, could you please get up!" Jesus she has a huge ass on her. Thought the officer as he looked at Niece laying in the bed. Then his radio went off and the noise caused Niece to open her eyes. She jumped up when she saw the police standing over her.

"What's going on? Why are you here?" Niece covered her body with the covers off of the bed.

"Calm down ma'am! There was a call for a break-in at this address. I'm gonna go to the front while you put on some clothes." The officer walked out of the bedroom and Niece scrambled out of the bed to put some clothes on. What the fuck is he talking about a break-in, thought Niece as she put on some boyshorts and a t-shirt. After she got dressed, she walked to the front room.

"Ma'am, the front door was open when I got here. Could you check to see if there is anything missing." Niece began looking around while she called Sweet's phone. When Niece saw that the cookie jars were on the counter and they were empty, she damn near choked.

"Somebody broke in while I was asleep and they stole our money!" Niece was now crying. Sweets had to fight herself from laughing while she listened to Niece crying on the speaker phone. She had to make herself get serious.

"What the fuck do you mean Niece?! Oh my God, what are

we gonna do now? How in the fuck did you not wake up? Bitch you're lying!" Sweets played as is she knew nothing.

"I swear, the police woke me up." Cried Niece.

"I'm at the hospital with Drop. I'll be home when he goes home. File a fuckin police report."

"Okay, I'm so__" Sweets hung up before Niece could finish her sentence.

"You're ah dog ass bitch, just like yo mami!" Carl Lee told Sweets and they burst into laughter. While the laughed someone knocked on the door.

"Come in!" Drop yelled and Lil Tim came walking in the room with his arm in a sling.

"What's up my boy?" Drop said smiling glad to see Lil Tim was okay.

"Big bruh, I'm sorry. I don't want you to think that I would ever try to play you or cross you. You know my brother and you are like brothers. I got mad love for you bruh." Lil Tim explained hoping that Drop wasn't mad at him.

"Lil bruh, everything Gucci. I just want you to learn from your mistake and promise me that you're gonna kick yo habit." Drop hated the fact that Lil Tim was only nineteen and already gettin his nose dirty.

"On god big bruh. I got you. I'm done with that shit." Lil Tim promised Drop.

"My boy, I thought ya ass was dead the way you was laying on the ground bleeding and not moving."

"Hell naw! Bruh! I was playing dead." Said Lil Tim and everybody burst into laughter.

****

What the fuck am I doing here to speak on the behalf of somebody I don't know, thought Candy as she sat in the hallway of the Parole board building. The door to the conference room came open and a white woman that works for the state came in.

"Is there anyone here to speak on the behalf of Sonya Mitchell?" Said the lady. Here goes nothing, thought Candy as she raised her hand.

"Yes ma'am! I am" Said Candy.

"And you are?"

"Candice Watts, her daughter." The lady wrote Candy's name down then walked her into the conference room where the board members were seated. Candy walked in front of the parole board looking professional in a black two-piece business suit.

"This is Candice Watts, the daughter of Sonya Mitchell." The lady presented Candice to the board.

"Ma'am please tell us why we should consider granting Sonya Mitchell parole." Said one of the members of the board. Candy took a deep breath.

"I feel as if my mother has rehabilitated and has become a better person during her time of incarceration. It would be a pleasure to have her home with her family so we can enjoy this newfound spirit that has overcome her and blessed her to find a relationship with God. I feel that she can and will help others to become a better person by living a positive life." Candy shocked herself with her choice of words. A few of the board members looked at one another then shuffled through some papers. An older looking white man on the board stamped a paper sitting in front of him with the word GRANTED in big red letters.

"Your mother will be released two weeks from today on supervised parole. You make sure she reports to her P.O. and does the right thing when she gets home. She is lucky to have a smart, young lady like you in her life. Erica Dawson is next." Said the older white man and Candy was escorted out of the conference room. Oh my God I did it, thought Candy as she walked out of the parole building dialing Drop's phone number.

"What's up bay?" Drop answered the phone as he climbed into Car Lee's car.

"Mama will be released in two weeks." Candy told him.

"Damn bay, that's what's up. Thanks so much for everything baby. Ya baby mama made parole." Drop told Carl Lee.

"Got damn! It's turn up time." Yelled Carl Lee.

"Bay, I'ma be at home waitin on you. Be safe on that highway."

"Okay. I'll be there in about three hours."

"Bay."

"Yeah Bay!"

"I love you Candice!"

"I love you Ivan!" Drop hung up the phone with Candy and he called Sweets

"Yeah!" Sweets answered the phone with an attitude.

"Yo mama made parole." Drop informed her.

"Fuck that bitch. That stank hoe ain't got shit comin from me and she betta stay the fuck away from me and my child." Sweets hated Sonya. It started when Sweets and Drop were young, but the icing got put on the cake while Sweets was pregnant. Sonya was supposed to drive Sweets car to the store to get some tampons, but she got on some geek monster shit and rented Sweet's car to some lil niggas in Northwood Projects for some crack and the lil nigga wrecked Sweets car, totalling it out. Sweets hadn't fucked wit Sonya since then.

"I see you still holdin on to that old shit!" Drop didn't like the fact that his sister and mama weren't on speaking terms. Drop hated a lot of shit his mom did in the past, but he always forgave her because he knew his mama had a gorilla on her back that she couldn't seem to shake for shit.

"If that's what you called me for I gotta go. I love you." Sweets hung up on Drop. She didn't feel like hearing shit about Sonya.

****

"Ooh, fuck me! Give me that big black cock." Kira heard someone say and she opened her eyes to find JB fucking some skinny ass white girl with big titties and blond hair. JB had the white girl bent over on the chair next to the bed, fucking her from the back. Kira jumped out of the bed and threw on some clothes. Then she grabbed her car keys and cell phone so she could leave, but when she got close to the room door, she was met by JB's fist. JB punched Kira so hard in the face that she dropped everything out of her hands and fell to the floor.

"Agghh, hmmm!" Cried Kira. When she opened her eyes one of them remained shut and she felt extreme pain in it. Her eye was hurting so bad all she could do was hold it while she cried. JB grabbed Kira by her hair and pulled her into the bed.

"Stop JB! Please stop!" Kira cried

"Shut up, bitch! You wanted ya pussy ate so you bout to get it ate. Shelly eat this hoe pussy!" Shelley walked to the bed and tried to take Kira shorts off, but Kira slapped her hand away from her. JB clamped his hands around Kira's throat.

"Bitch, take yo shorts off and open yo legs!" JB demanded Kira, with thick white spit flying from his mouth. Kira didn't want to get hit again, plus she couldn't breathe so she quickly done as she was told. As soon as Kira took of her shorts and spread her legs, JB stopped choking her and Shelley started eating her pussy like it was the last supper.

Kira's eye was hurting so bad that she just wanted something to take the pain away. She looked at the nightstand next to her and saw the bag of cocaine. She grabbed the bag and sniffed it, while she lay on her back getting her breast sucked by JB and her pussy ate by Shelley, Kira felt her pain melting away instantly. It wasn't a minute later before she put her hand on top of shelley's head and started gyrating her hips as she enjoyed Shelley's mouth game.

"Ahhh, umm, aahh!" Moaned Kira. JB was having his first

threesome and he was loving every moment of it. He stopped sucking on Kira's titties and laid back in the bed.

"Both of y'all come suck this dick!" JB grabbed the last of the cocaine from Kira and poured it on the head of his dick. Kira and Shelley sniffed the cocaine off his dick and then they started suckin and slobbing all over his meat stick. JB was loving his menage trois. Kira backed off the dick as she watched Shelley go numb on the dick. Shelley started licking under JB's nut sack.

"Ooh ooh shit yeah! Bitch, lick that shit!" JB had fell in love with the way Shelley got his dick hard when they had first made it to the room. JB cocked his legs back like a bitch and Shelley started eating his ass hole. What the fuck? Oh hell no, thought Kira.

"Kira lick that shit!" Kira looked at JB like he was crazy.

"No, I ain't___" was all Kira got out her mouth before JB grabbed her by her hair like a ragdoll and stuffed her face in his ass, clinging her head against Shelley's head. Shelley moved back so Kira could fulfill JB's wishes. Kira couldn't believe what she was about to do as she stuck her tongue out and licked JB's asshole.

"Ahh, yeah baby! Lick that shit!" Kira couldn't believe she was licking JB's hairy, nasty ass hole that he hadn't washed in days. She felt like she was about to puke, so she got up and ran to the bathroom where she threw up everywhere. JB was gonna go drag Kira from the bathroom, but he heard her vomiting. Shelley was glad Kira was out of her way so she could finish turning JB out. Kira washed her mouth and got herself together then she peeked out the door to see what was goin on in the room without her.

"Ooh ahh yess baby!" JB was moaning like a bitch with his legs in the air like a stripper.

Slurp Slurp Slurp

Shelley got JB's ass hole soaking wet while she stroked his hard dick. Here goes nothing, thought Shelley, and she stuck the tip of her index finger inside JB's asshole. What the fuck, thought Kira as she watched Shelley stick her finger in JB's asshole. The part that surprised her the most is that JB loved it.

"Ooh, shit baby, yes, yes, yes!" JB screamed as he came harder than he ever came in his life. His legs trembled while Shelley continued to penetrate him with more of her finger.

"You like that, don't you daddy!" Shelley knew she had JB right where she wanted him. She licked his cum off of her hand then climbed on top of him and kissed him in the mouth.

"Ehmm, hmm! Baby you make daddy feel so good." JB whimpered like a hoe.

"I'm always gonna make daddy feel good!" Kira couldn't believe her eyes and ears. This fiasco had made her sick, but JB had made her even sicker. The pain in Kira's face came back and harder than before. She walked out of the bathroom to get the sack of powder, but it was empty.

"Jeremy, the stuff is gone and I need some because my face is hurting bad as hell!" JB laid in the bed like he didn't hear Kira.

"I got something even better for you girl." Shelley jumped

off the bed and grabbed her purse. Shelly pulled out a brown paper bag and poured the contents in the bag onto the bed. Kira was lost to what Shelley was doing. It looked like Shelley was building something as Kira watched her take the rose out of the glass tube and stuffed the end of the glass tube with brillo. Then Shelley pulled out a sack of white rocks from her purse. They looked like diamonds to Kira. Shelley took one of the rocks and put it on top of the end of the glass tube that had the brillo stuffed in it. She put the opposite end in her mouth and lit fire to the rock while she sucked the smoke from the glass tube which is now considered to be a crack pipe or a glass dick. Shelley took the pipe away from her mouth, inhaled deeply, the blew the smoke out.

That shit stinks, thought Kira as Shelley handed her the pipe then placed a fresh rock on top of it. Kira did as she saw Shelley do and she hit the pipe. When she inhaled, she instantly got higher than she ever imagined she could get. Kira started hearing noises and felt like somebody or something was coming to get her. She dropped the pipe on the bed and ran to the window peeping out of the blinds. Then she ran to the bathroom and washed her face. When she walked back in the room JB and Shelley were sitting up in the bed naked smoking crack.

"Girl, sit yo ass down, you just high!" JB saw how big Kira's eyes were. Kira sat on the bed. Shelley crawled over to Kira and started kissing her. JB, Shelley and Kira smoked crack and freaked all day long.

CHAPTER 5

Sweets decided not to work tonight. She sat at the bar of the Player's Club and enjoyed a few drinks while she watched the thirsty bitches that worked at the club slave for the almighty dollar. She wasn't ever hurting for money because she grinded hard and always saved her money. The ten bands she took from Niece was blow money. Sweets made Niece pay for disrespecting her.

Every nigga or bitch that came to the bar couldn't help but to gawk at Sweets as she sat at the bar looking edible in a Kim Wooo body dress that bear hugged her curves. She had Red Bottoms on her feet and her Gucci Guilty perfume made the onlookers want Sweets even more when her scent filled their nostrils. Sweets even had to compliment herself cause she knew she was murdering the scene. Every time Sweets looked towards the stage, Niece was all in her mouth as she conversated with different individuals at the bar. Is you big mad or little mad?, thought Sweets as she licked the salt off the rim of her glass, flirting with the dude she was talking to.

Fat Rabbit and his crew walked in the club stuntin like they were super on, talking loud and flashin wads of money to try to grab the attention of anyone who would pay them any attention. When Fat Rabbit saw Sweets looking so damn good, he damn near lost his mind. She had really fucked his head up the night before. He wanted her so bad that he could taste her. Fat Rabbit had the audacity to pull up on Sweets while she was already indulged in a conversation with somebody.

"What's up, sexy?" Sweets turned her head in Fat Rabbit's direction.

"Don't you see that I am talking to somebody, with yo disrespectful ass!" Sweets rolled her eyes and sucked her teeth as she turned her attention back to the dude she was talking to. Fat Rabbit felt like he had just got clowned in front of his homeboys.

"Ahh! Nigga, you just got dissed!" Screamed one of Fat Rabbit's partners. Fat Rabbit didn't have a rebound for the shot that he had just missed and he was pissed.

"Bitch, who you think you talkin to?" Fat Rabbit grabbed Sweets by her arm and snatched her up from the stool she was sitting on.

"Nigga, you betta get yo fuckin' hands off me!" Sweets hollered, but Fat Rabbit picked her up and took her into the restroom so he'd have time to beat her ass before security kicked the door down.

"Nah, bitch, you gonna learn how to talk to a man." Fat Rabbit threw Sweets into the restroom wall then locked the door. Security made it to the door twenty seconds too late. On her knees on the floor, Sweets reached inside her bra and got her box cutter. As soon as she flicked the blade out Fat Rabbit drew his fist back to punch Sweets in her face, but he was too slow. Sweets swung and sliced Fat Rabbit's face with the box cutter.

"Aghhh! Aghhh!" Fat Rabbit let loose of Sweets and grabbed his face which was gushing blood from the cut. Sweets scrambled to the door and opened it.

"Oh, shit!! Get her in my office and get that nigga out of my club." Screamed Big Toney, when he saw Fat Rabbit leaking blood all over the restroom.

"I'ma kill you, bitch!" Fat Rabbit screamed as the security toted him out of the club in the Full Nelson.

"Fuck you, weak ass nigga!" Sweets hollered back before the security closed the office door.

"Y'all niggas wit him, y'all gotta go too!" Big Toney told the dudes who came in with Fat Rabbit.

"Come on Big Man! We ain't got nothing to do with that shit. That nigga got what he deserved fa putting his hands on a woman. We came to party and spend some money." Weezy told Big Toney because he wasn't ready to leave. He had just laid eyes on Niece's fat ass.

"Aight, but I'm letting you know now, if you start any shit you won't like the outcome!" Big Toney was mad as hell that Fat Rabbit had put his dick beaters on Sweets. Big Toney had held a secret crush on Sweets since he first laid eyes on her.

"We got you Big Man! We on some chill shit. Straight up!" Weezy was glad that they didn't have to leave.

"Smoove! Clean up all this got damn blood! It look like Freddy Kruger been in this muthafucka." Smoove, the crackhead that was the janitor at the club, rushed to get the mop and some towels to clean up the blood with.

"I can't believe that Fat fuck put his fuckin' hands on me." Sweets paced back and forth in Big Tony's small office space. She was mad as hell. Her Red Bottoms were scuffed up and she had two broken finger nails. Sweets rubbed the back of her head and she felt a small knot. That must've happened when that bitch nigga threw me in tha bathroom, thought Sweets. Big Toney came into the office.

"I gotta call ya brother and let him know what just happened." Big Toney picked up his phone to call Drop.

"No, Toney! Drop just got shot last night. He don't need to get in anymore bullshit right now!" Sweets knew Drop was gonna be on some murda murda, kill kill shit about her.

"Who tha fuck shot nephew?" Big Toney knew nothing about Drop getting shot.

"That lil geeked out nigga that girl Magic who work here go with. He shot Baby G's lil brother, Lil Tim and he shot Drop. That nigga took Drop's chain, a quarter of soft, and a few bands." Sweets stayed in the office for thirty minutes talking to Big Toney and Fantasy, one of the strippers.

That bitch ain't even came to check on me, thought Sweets as she walked out of Big Toney's office. When she walked to the back of the club, she saw Niece sitting in Weezy's lap, talking and laughing. I got something for this bitch, thought Sweets. Then she got one of the security dudes to walk her to her car. Her phone rang as soon as she got in her car. It was Drop.

"Hello!"

"You handled ya business, didn't ya?" Drop was laying in Candy's lap eating grapes with the phone on speaker.

"I tried to slice that Fat bitch's throat but I hit him in the face." Sweets pulled out of the club parking lot.

"Look! Don't go back to that fuckin' club until I handle that fat fuck nigga, ya hear me! And where yo strap at?"

"I got it! It was in my purse. The shit happened so fast. I couldn't get to it!" Drop knew if Sweets would've gotten to her gun, Fat Rabbit ass would be dead, but now he was gonna have to handle the nigga's funeral arrangements.

"Alright! Bring me my nephew in the morning."

"Hey, sis!" Candy screamed in the background.

"What's up, bitch! Bout to go put yo friends shit out on the porch. Don't you know that hoe ain't even come check on me? She can find her somewhere to go tonight though, cause I'm going back to dick." Drop and Candy burst into laughter.

"You know you yo mama's child, bye girl!" Drop hung up. Sweets hated the fact that Fat Rabbit had put his hands on her. She knew her brother and she knew he was gonna kill Fat Rabbit as soon as he could. When Sweets got home, she did exactly what she told Candy she was about to do. She threw all Niece's belongings into trash bags and sat the bags on the front porch. Afterwards, Sweets ran herself some hot bath water and took a long, relaxing bubble bath while she read "The G In Game," a new urban novel.

"I wish I could stay with you too Weezy. But I can't", Niece told Weezy on the phone as she pulled up at home.

"Damn, Lil baby, you had ah nigga shit rock hard all night." Niece giggled cause she had felt Weezy's erection when she was dancing on him at the club.

"If I can slip away, I will call you, but I gotta go!" Niece hung up the phone as she got out of the car. She was about to stick her key into the lock until she saw the paper with her name wrote on it in big letters sitting on top of three trash bags. What the fuck is this, thought Niece. Then she looked inside one of the bags. No this bitch didn't! Niece got mad as hell and tried to unlock the door, but the deadbolt lock was on.

"Open the fucking door, Sweets!" Niece yelled as she knocked on the door. After five minutes of knocking, Niece knew Sweets wasn't gonna open the door for her, so she packed her bags into her car. With nowhere else to go, Niece called Weezy.

"What it do, lil baby?" Said Weezy when he answered the phone.

"You wanna meet me somewhere?" Niece pulled out of the apartment complex knowing exactly why Sweets put her out. She couldn't even be mad at Sweets.

"Shid, lil baby, I'm at the LaQuinta behind Waffle House on University. Room 217." Weezy was glad than ah muthafucka that Niece called him back because he was just scrolling on Snapchat looking for a bitch he could pay to fuck.

"Okay, I'll be there in about eight minutes."

"Bet!" Weezy looked at his phone and saw that his homeboy Blue was calling so he clicked over.

"What's up, son son!" Weezy started making up the bed that he had been fucking in already earlier that day.

"Shit my boy! I got Marquita with me and we bout to pull up." Said Blue.

"You got some Molly?" Weezy asked Blue.

"Hell yeah! She fire too!"

"Bring some shells too!" They hung up. Weezy knew Marquita was with whatever and he knew if he put Niece on the Molly then she would be with whatever also. Minutes later Niece knocked on Weezy's room door carrying an overnight bag in her hand.

"What's up lil baby?" Weezy let Niece in the room. Damn that ass fat, thought Weezy when Niece walked past him.

"Nothing! Can I take a shower?"

"Yeah, but let's smoke ah blunt first, my partna and my home girl bout to pull up."

"Okay!" Niece sat on the bed.

"You want a drink?" Weezy needed to get loose.

"What you got?"

"Jose Cuervo and some Coronas."

"You got some juice?" Niece didn't drink straight liquor.

"Yeah!" Weezy opened the refrigerator and grabbed the cranberry juice. As soon as he shut the refrigerator there was a knock at the door. Weezy looked through the peephole and saw it was Blue and Marquita, so he opened the door for them to come in.

"What's up my boy?" Blue stepped into the room and looked at Niece like she was Filet Mignon.

"Not shit my boy! Niece this Blue, Marquita this is Niece. Marquita was 5'8" in height and 160 in weight. She was a thick, redbone with tattoos all over her body and a pair of big pretty lips. Marquita wore her hair finger length and dyed purple. She was known to have the best head in the city. Marquita smiled at Niece.

"Hey boo." Marquita spoke to Niece trying to remember where she had seen her.

"Hey, wasn't you at the Players Club the other night?" Niece could not forget Marquita's hair, piercings and tattoos.

"I thought I remembered your face from somewhere." Weezy and Blue mixed up drinks while Niece and Marquita talked. They poured three grams of Molly into the bottle of Jose Cuervo. Then they mixed the liquor with cranberry juice and poured it on ice. This remedy had always worked for them whenever it came to them getting a freak session started. The four of them smoked blunts, drank liquor and politiced about all types of shit. It was about thirty minutes later when Niece felt an euphoric feeling sweep over her body and she needed to take a shit. She went to the bathroom and locked the door.

Cluke   Cluke   Cluke

Niece dropped three big ass turds before she even sat down

good on the toilet. A midst of sweat appeared on her forehead and she fiend for a cigarette. Damn I need a cigarette, thought Niece.

"Marquita, bring me a cigarette!" When Weezy and Blue heard Niece they knew she was high. Marquita fixed up a cigarette and went to the bathroom door, but it was locked.

"Hold on!" Marquita told Niece as she picked the lock.

"Girl, put some water on that shit!" Marquita frowned up her face when she opened the door and the smell hit her hard. Niece flushed the toilet.

"Thanks girl! Niece grabbed the cigarette from Marquita and pulled it so hard with her lips that the fire became longer than the cigarette.

"I gotta shit too!" Marquita already knew that they had put Molly in the liquor.

"I'm almost done! Will you brang my bag from in there?" Niece threw the cigarette into the toilet and started wiping her ass while Marquita got her overnight bag for her. When Marquita brought Niece her bag, she got butt naked. Damn that pussy fat, thought Marquita as she sat down on the toilet to take a shit. Marquita reached out and gripped Niece's ass.

"Damn that ass soft too boo!" Marquita licked her lips.

"This pussy sweet too!" Niece told Marquita then she stepped into the shower. I'm surely gonna find out, thought Marquita. As soon as she got done shitting, she stripped butt naked and got into the shower with Niece.

"Can I wash that sweet pussy for you baby?" Marquita

grabbed the soap and rag from Niece.

"You can do what you wanna do!" Niece was feeling freaky and she could look at Marquita and tell that she knew how to please her pussy. Marquita lathered the rag and washed Niece's body from her neck to her breast. When she got down to Niece's pussy, she got down on her knees so that she was eye-level with Niece's pretty pussy lips. Marquita parted Niece's pussy lips and washed her thoroughly.

"Ummm….wash that pussy baby!" Niece propped her foot up on the side of the tub so Marquita could get in all of her cracks.

"Dem hoes probably in there freakin' my boy!" Blue said. He was super geeked off the Molly.

"Shid, my boy. Let's go see!" Weezy led the way into the bathroom with his Iphone in his hand on video record. Weezy pulled back the shower curtain and Marquita and Niece were tongue kissing while they played with one another's pussy under the shower water. Blue pulled out his phone and started recording the beautiful scene also. Minutes later the girls got out of the shower and went into the room where Weezy and Blue took turns fucking both girls all morning long. At six that morning, Blue went to the bathroom to piss. When he released his piss, it burnt so bad that he had to cut his piss off immediately.

"Aghh fuck!" Blue grunted lowly as he held his burning dick in his hand. Damn, that hoe burnt me the other day, thought Blue as he released his piss a little bit at a time trying to minimize the pain from burning so bad.

CHAPTER 6

Candy rolled over to cuddle with her man, but to her surprise Drop wasn't in the bed. When she rolled back over something beneath her made a crunching noise. Candy smiled from ear to ear when she saw the dozen roses that were behind her. She was about to get out of the bed when her phone rang. She looked at the caller ID and saw that it was Kira's mother calling.

"Hello." Candy answered.

"Hi, Candice!"

"Hey, Mama Brown."

"Have you seen my child? I've been calling her phone for two days now and I still haven't gotten an answer." Candy didn't know what to tell Kira's mother, but she could hear the worry in the woman's voice.

"Naw, Mama Brown, I haven't seen or talked to her, but I can call around if you want me to."

"Would you do that for me? I just wanna know that she's alive. She has been lying to me for the past few months like she was gonna go with me to see her sister at the prison, but she ain't went yet." Miss Brown didn't know where she went wrong with her twin girls, but she definitely went wrong somewhere.

"Let me call around and I'll call you back in a minute."

"Thanks Hunny" They hung up and Candy called Kira's phone.

"Hey girl!" Kira sounded groggy and dry.

"Bitch, I know you see your mama calling your phone, so why you not answering?"

"Candy, I can't let my mama see me like this, plus she just wants me to go with her to see Lay Kira and I don't fuck with that hoe in no shape, form or fashion."

"What the fuck you mean let her see you like what? What's wrong? Bitch, where you at? I'm bout to come get you!" Candy was concerned. She knew Kira was somewhere with JB who was hiding cause he figured Drop's and Lil Tim's people were looking for him which they were. That's why Candy really wanted to go get Kira.

"No Candy, I can't!" Kira hung up the phone and started examining her face in the bathroom mirror. Her face was blue and purple around her eye. I do need to let mama know that I'm straight so she won't be worried about me, thought Kira then called her mama.

Candy couldn't believe that Kira had hung up on her. She got out of the bed and her phone rang again. Fuck, thought Candy when she saw her boyfriend Antonio's name on the caller ID. He was locked up in South Carolina for a murder charge. He had a cell phone in the County Jail, but he could only use it when certain CO's would charge it up for him. Candy had been ducking his calls since she started talking to Drop, but she continued to send him money.

When she did talk to him, she would say she was in class or working when he called and that's why she didn't answer the previous time he called. She for damn sure wasn't about to chance answering the phone now when she didn't know where Drop was at. As soon as her phone stopped ringing, it started ringing again. It was Mama Brown.

"Miss Brown I," Candy started to say but Mama Brown interrupted.

"It's okay, baby. I talked to her. She said she's okay. Candy please watch my baby for me if you can!" Candy was relieved that Kira called her mom.

"I will do my best, Mama Brown. You be careful!"

"Okay hunny, you do the same." They hung up

I need to call Tonio back and tell him that it's over. I don't want to hurt him while he's down though. What am I gonna do? Candy questioned herself as she walked to the front room wearing the t-shirt and shorts she went to sleep in. Candy couldn't believe that her and Drop had been talking for over a month, she had damn near moved in with him, but they still hadn't had sex. Maybe that's why I'm not over Tonio yet, thought Candy as she looked at Carl Lee who shot Drop a we've got company look, causing Drop to stop talking.

"There's my daughter!" Carl Lee tried to change the subject.

"Nah, don't hush when I come in here. What ya'll talking about? I wanna know!" Drop looked at Candy and shook his head.

"Nope bay! Can't do! The less you know, the better off you

are" Drop didn't want Candy in his business.

"So I guess you lied when you told me that whatever is yours is mines as well!" Candy had a mug on her face cause she hated to be lied to. Carl Lee looked at Drop.

"Damn, she good!" Carl Lee couldn't even deny her response. Drop shook his head and then looked at Candy.

"Come here!" Drop pulled Candy down onto the couch he was sitting on and he looked her in the eyes.

"Look, I've gotten shot and ah nigga done put his hands on my sista in the same week. I ain't no hoe! I wasn't raised to let shit like that ride. I gotta handle my business bay!" Drop was ready to kill JB and Fat Rabbit. He didn't give a fuck about healing up.

"Your beef is my hamburger! I'm gonna handle both of them niggas and you're gonna sit your ass at home and heal." Drop and Carl Lee looked at Candy like she was crazy.

"Damn! She's better than good. She's great! I now pronounce you husband and wife!" Shouted Carl Lee. Candy leaned over to Drop and stuck her tongue into his mouth. They kissed for a minute before they were interrupted by Carl Lee.

"Mane, got damn! Save that shit for the honeymoon!" Drop and Candy burst into laughter.

"Come on Mane, pay me so I can leave and go get those number nines that came out today." Carl Lee kept the newest Jordans. Candy looked at Carl Lee and twisted up her face.

"Carl Lee don't no number nines come out today!" Said Candy.

"See, baby girl. That's where you wrong at. My man Abdula down at Northside Quick Stop got a new shipment in this morning. Now come on Drop, before he sell out." Drop damn near died laughing so hard at Carl Lee talking about the bootleg man at the corner store. Drop gained his composure and gave Carl Lee four-hundred dollars.

"I'm gone now! Ya'll gone and make me a grandbaby!" Candy couldn't stop laughing at Carl Lee as he walked out the door.

"Yo daddy is a damn fool!"

"Shid, what's mine is yours, remember? So he's yours too!" Drop and Candy started laughing. Drop stopped laughing and got serious.

"Bay, I don't want you to get in any trouble. I'm gonna handle…" Before Drop could say another word, Candy covered his mouth with her hand.

"I'm gonna handle them niggas, bay! You are a convicted felon. I have a clean record, so if I was to get caught, my punishment would be less harsh because I haven't been in trouble before. Anyways, bay, you know niggas think with they dick so that Fat Rabbit nigga gonna be super easy.' Drop stared at Candy as she talked and he could tell by her choice of words that she had fucked with a street nigga before. Candy stopped talking and stood up from the couch. Drop watched as Candy stripped down butt naked. Damn bay, thought Drop, as he looked at Candy's pretty plump pussy staring at him. Candy licked her lips seductively at Drop . Then she started walking towards the bedroom. She was tired of waiting on Drop to make the first move. Now Candy was finna throw the pussy on him.

****

Kira sat in the bathroom for thirty minutes after she got off the phone with her mama. She couldn't believe the shit she was doing, but Kira wanted more drugs and more sex. She had created a monster inside of her body and the monster was making all the decisions for Kira. She looked in the mirror and she didn't know if the swelling was goin down in her face or if she was losing weight. Kira had only been smoking crack for twenty four hours but she could already see and feel the difference in her appearance.

"Kira!" She heard Shelley scream her name. Kira walked into the room where Shelley was at fixing up the glass dick.

"This the last of it baby!" Shelley hit the pipe then she passed it to Kira, who finished off the rock. As soon as Kira hit the pipe, paranoia set off in her and she went to peek out of the blinds. For some reason, her high only lasted for three minutes.

"Why don't I feel it anymore?" Kira asked Shelley.

"Because what you just hit was only a wake-up. We need to get some more. I know who has that straight drop too!" Shelley knew Carl Lee had that drop head.

"Call him!" Kira told Shelley, then she went in JB's pockets while he was sleep and pulled out all of his money. JB only had six hundred dollars left from the money he robbed Drop for. Kira gave Shelley the whole six hundred and Shelley called Carl Lee.

"What's up, bitch?" Carl Lee answered the phone while he

pumped his gas at the Northside Quick Stop.

"Hey Daddy! I need some drop, can you get me some?" Since Drop had gotten shot, Carl Lee was handling all the business so he was on deck with the straight drop.

"You got some money, bitch?"

"Of course Daddy! Bring me something for the six hundred!"

"Bitch you ballin ain't ya! Where you at?" Carl Lee jumped in his car.

"At the King's Inn, room 224."

"Alright, give me twenty minutes!" Carl Lee headed to the stash spot to get some work.

"He said he'll be here in twenty minutes. Let's go to Burger King and get some chew. Girl, you gotta eat when you smoke this shit or you'll lose your weight fast as hell." Shelley and Kira went to Burger King, leaving JB at the room sleep.

Carl Lee pulled up at the King's Inn bumping the Migos song "Handsome and Wealthy," from his car system while he counted the money laying in his lap. Shelley and Kira pulled in the parking space beside him right when he was about to call Shelley's phone to tell her he was outside. *I know got damn well she ain't smokin' no yams! She too fine*, thought Carl Lee when he saw Kira get out of her car. He quickly rolled down his window.

"Aye lil baby!" Kira looked in Carl Lee's direction.

"Yeah, you! Come here." Carl Lee motioned for Kira to come to him.

"Jump in the front seat Kira!" Said Shelley as she jumped in the back seat of Carl Lee's car. Kira got in the front seat.

"Damn, Shelley! You been holding back from daddy ain't you?" Carl Lee was intrigued by how fine Kira was even though she had a black eye.

"No daddy! I just met her yesterday!" Shelley reached around the seat and handed Carl Lee the money for the dope. Carl Lee couldn't help from lusting over Kira's sexy body and pretty brown skin.

"Do you get down, lil baby?" Carl Lee had to know if Kira smoked cause if she did he was about to trick off on her.

"Yeah, I just started yesterday tho!" Kira giggled. Carl Lee couldn't believe what he'd just heard. Just when Carl Lee was about to put his game down, the door to the room flew open and caught everybody in the cars attention. Kira got scared to death as she watched JB walk to the passenger side of Carl Lee's car and opened the door.

"Bitch, what you doin' in this nigga's car?" JB grabbed Kira by her hair, snatched her out of the car, and drug her into the hotel room.

"Here bich! Get this shit and get out my car so I can leave this hot ass hotel. If you and lil mama get away from that nigga call me and I'll come get y'all" Carl Lee told Shelley as he handed her the dope.

"Okay daddy! I'll call you later on." Shelley grabbed the dope and jumped out of Carl lee's car. When she walked into the room, JB was whooping Kira with a belt like she was a child. Kira was balled up in the bed crying while he hit her with the belt.

"JB, stop hittin' that girl and come hit you some of this good dope so you can calm down." It was like Shelley had mind control over JB because right then he threw down the belt and went and sat next to Shelley on the bed.

"Put me a big rock up there baby, I need to get high!" Jb said with heavy breathing. He loved smoking rocks. While he smoked Shelley fixed Kira a pipe.

"Here, baby! This will take the pain away!" Shelley handed Kira the glass dick and Kira immediately sat up in the bed to start smoking. She forgot about everything that had just happened as soon as she hit the dope.

For two weeks straight, all Shelley, JB and Kira did was smoke crack. JB even made kira and Shelley sell pussy using Craigslist and Snapchat. Sometimes when the tricks came to the room to fuck Kira or Shelley, JB would go into the bathroom or leave until they were finished. A few times JB burst into the room acting like the mad boyfriend and rob the trick for all of his money. The trick would be so scared that he would leave the room naked, leaving behind his wallet and clothes.

CHAPTER 7

Every since Sweets sliced Fat Rabbit in the face, him and his lil sisters had been on Snapchat and Facebook live talking shit about what they were gonna do to Sweets and Drop. Drop was mad for not goin' ahead and handlin' the situation as soon as it popped off, but Candy refused to let Drop leave the house for anything until he was one hundred percent. That's why Candy was sitting at the bar of the Player's Club on this Sunday night dressed in a white Chanel body dress that hugged her curves with a pair of white Chanel heels to match. Every nigga that came in the club tried to get Candy while she sat at the bar drinking on a club soda. Candy hadn't been to the club since Drop had gotten shot, but tonight she was on a mission. Candy had got word from one of the strippers that Fat Rabbit had been coming in the club every night looking for Sweets, so she figured he would probably drop in tonight.

At 12:15 a.m. Fat Rabbit came strolling through the doors of the Player's Club looking like he was looking for a specific someone. He scanned the club, but his eyes quickly came to a halt when he saw Candy sitting at the bar. Fat Rabbit quickly aborted his mission and approached Candy at the bar.

"What's up lil baby?" Candy damn near gagged from the smell of Fat Rabbit's breath, but she held her composure because she had shit to do. Candy turned in Fat Rabbit's direction and smiled. Damn Sweets fucked him up, thought Candy when she saw the cut on Fat Rabbit's face.

"Hey handsome!" Candy said smiling. This wasn't her first time to try to seduce someone. Candy had played as the bait one time for her boyfriend who was locked up. She helped him rob some trap niggas in her hometown, Charleston, South Carolina.

"Shid, my girl. What ah nigga like me gotta do to get with something as sexy as you?" Fat Rabbit was raping Candy with his eyes and assaulting her with his breath.

"If you get a room, let me tie you up and ride them fat lips of yourns, then we might can make something happen." Candy ran her tongue across her teeth. She had heard from a source that Fat Rabbit likes to eat pussy.

"Shid, my girl. What we waitin' on. Let's go!" Fat Rabbit was eager to leave the club with Candy. His dumb ass never thought that I'm Drops bitch, thought Candy as she got up from the bar. She walked out of the club with Fat Rabbit drooling on her heels. Candy had to stop herself from turning around and slapping the shit out of Fat Rabbit when he gripped her ass.

"I'll follow you to the room!" Candy told Fat Rabbit.

"Okay, lil baby. I'm going to the La Quinta on University." Fat Rabbit jumped in his Roxy Blue seventy-seven Chevy Caprice that sat on twenty-eight inch Forgiatos. He tried to blow the motor up in his car getting to the hotel. On his way to the hotel, not once did he think Candy was behind him on the phone with her man.

"Hey bay!"

"What's wrong? You sound nervous, beautiful!" Drop heard the odd tone in Candy's voice.

"Bay, we on the way to the La Quinta on University." Candy was getting more nervous by the second.

"Which one?" Candy was making Drop mad and she didn't even know it.

"I don't know yet!"

"Damn bay! You ain't ready for this type of shit!"

"Baby, I'm sorry!" Candy was nutting up on the mission. She began to doubt if she had what it took to pull the trigger of the baby 40 caliber glock that was inside her purse to kill Fat Rabbit once they got inside the hotel room.

"Mane, fuck! Call me and let me know what room y'all pull up to. I'm on my way to University right now!" Drop hung up the phone mad as hell. I knew better than to put this bitch in my business, thought Drop as he called Carl Lee while he ran outside to get into Candy's car. Since she was about to do some dirt, Drop had rented her a car to drive.

"What's up baby?" Carl Lee announced.

"Where you at?" Drop jumped into Candy's car and sat his 44 bulldog on his lap.

"I'm just rotating." Carl Lee knew something was wrong by the tone Drop was talking in.

"You strapped?"

"Nah, why? What's up?"

"Fuck! Nevermind!" Drop hung up the phone and floored the gas pedal on Candy's Camry. He sped through the curves of Monte Sano Mounting heading to University Drive. Three minutes later Candy called Drop's phone.

"Where the fuck you at?" Candy knew Drop was mad as hell by the way he was talking.

"We turning into the LaQuinta Inn across the street from Olive Garden on University!" Drop hung up on Candy.

One minute later Drop turned into the parking lot of the hotel and saw Fat Rabbit standing outside the door of the rental car, Candy was inside. Drop turned into the first parking space he saw and parked. By the time he got out of the car Fat Rabbit and Candy were walking towards the entrance of the hotel lobby. Fuck, thought Drop as he started joggin' to catch up with them before they made it to the entrance door of the hotel.

"Aye, fuck nigga!" Drop yelled to get Fat Rabbit's attention. Drop didn't want to do some coward shit by shooting Fat Rabbit in his back. Fat Rabbit turned around and his heart damn near jumped out of his chest when he saw Drop's 44 bulldog pointed at him. Fat Rabbit tried to reach for his gun and grab Candy for a shield at the same time, but he was too slow.

Clow Clow Clow

Drop fired three times hitting Fat Rabbit with every shot, dropping him to the ground. Drop tucked his revolver into his jeans and then ran back to the car he was driving and left the scene. Candy didn't know what to do when she saw people coming out of the hotel so she started screaming for someone to call an ambulance. Candy stayed till the police and ambulance came. After she left a short statement wit the police under a fake name and number, they let her leave. When Candy walked into the crib Drop was sitting on the couch smoking a blunt while he watched TV. The expression on Drop's face was unbearable for Candy to look at. She knew she had fucked up in a major way.

"Bay, I'm____" Candy started to say as she sat down next to Drop.

"Mane, don't say shit to me right now cause you some bullshit. You should've stayed the fuck out of my business in the first place." Drop got up from the couch, grabbed his keys to his donk and left out of the house. Candy sunk into the couch and started crying. She had wanted to prove her loyalty to Drop so bad, but she had only made the situation worse.

Drop drove through the city smoking Rapper weed with the top dropped on his donk listening to Future's song "It Will Never Be The Same No More." He had so much on his mind as he drove, that he didn't notice the Narcs that were behind him. Drop turned off Sparkman Drive onto Jordan and a new model Camaro sped in front of him. A Ram truck got behind him and then both vehicles hit their lights. Mane, fuck, thought Drop. Then he pulled into the parking lot of Club 47 and killed his engine. Drop watched the two black narcotics walk to his car. One of them going on each side of the car.

"Get out the car!" Agent Craigs told Drop. Drop knew Agent Craigs was crooked as they come and didn't mind whooping ah nigga ass so he didn't say anything. He just got out of the car.

"What you got on you?" Craigs asked Drop while the other narc started searching Drop's car from the passenger side.

"Do your job mane!" Was all the words Drop had for Craigs. He already knew how Craigs got down.

"Okay. Turn around and put your hands behind your back." Craigs said calmly.

"For what? I ain't did shit!" Drop knew Craigs was on some bullshit, just harassing him unless they knew about the shooting. Fuckin narcs wouldn't be pullin me over for a shooting, thought Drop as he put his hands behind his back to get cuffed.

"Uh oh! Look what we got here!" The other Narc pulled a freezer bag with 9 ounces of cocaine from under the passenger seat of Drop's Donk. Craigs slammed Drop to the ground and cuffed him.

"Mane, yall on some bullshit!" Growled Drop as Craigs and Wilson threw him in the back seat of the regular patrol car that pulled up. They took Drop to the Huntsville City Metro Jail and put him in the booking cell without a bond. Drop called Carl Lee's phone.

"Who in the fuck is this callin' me from the jail?" Carl Lee said when he accepted the call.

"This Drop!" Carl Lee's heart sank into the pit of his

stomach.

"What happened, baby?"

"The narcs planted some work in my car when they pulled me over." Carl Lee knew Drop was telling the truth because he wasn't the one doing the serving, Carl Lee was.

"How much is your bond?"

"They ain't gave me one. They got an investigating hold on me."

"So what you want me to do baby?"

"Call my lawyer in the morning and let him know what the deal is."

"Okay, baby! I love you!"

"Love you too!" Drop hung up the phone and called Candy.

"Bay what happened?" Said Candy when she accepted the call.

"Look, don't worry about me, just make sure you be in Montgomery in the morning to pick up my mama from prison at seven o'clock."

"Bay, what happened?" Candy cried into the phone, but Drop just hung up on her. Candy cried herself to sleep.

CHAPTER 8

"Baby, I'm gonna be waiting for you on the other side of that fence." Sonya told Lay Lay who only had two weeks till she got out.

"Okay baby. Please don't hurt me Sonya! I really love you." Lay Lay stared deeply into Sonya's eyes.

"I won't baby!" Sonya and Lay Lay hugged and kissed. When they released each other, Lay Lay started crying.

"Baby, you got my son's phone number and his address. That's where I'll be staying at. I will be in the house, not in the streets. Okay baby! Stop crying!" Sonya hated to leave Lay Lay, but she had to.

"Inmate Sonya Mitchell please report to the shift office with all of your property." The CO announced over the intercom.

"I gotta go, baby. I love you!"

"I love you, too!" Sonya and Lay Lay kissed and hugged then Sonya grabbed her property and went to the shift office.

When Sonya reached the shift office, she didn't see anyone she recognized to be there to pick her up. The CO in the shift office gave Sonya a bag containing shoes and clothes that someone had brought for her to wear home. Sonya went into the restroom and changed into the Victoria's Secret sweatsuit and new Air Max that was in the bag. Sonya walked out of the restroom and gave the CO the state prison uniform, then she signed her release papers. Candy watched Sonya sign her papers then start looking around for her ride.

"Are you ready?" Candy stood up from the chair she was sitting in, taking Sonya by surprise. Who is she, thought Sonya as she observed Candy from head to toe.

"Are you here to pick me up?" Sonya asked, wondering where did she know this sexy female from.

"Yes Miss Sweets! I'm Ivan's fiancee." That got Sonya's attention.

"Oh okay! Nice to meet you. Yeah, we can get the hell up out of here right now!" Sonya couldn't help but to acknowledge how fine Candy was as she walked behind Candy on the way to the car. When they got inside the car, Sonya saw how pretty Candy was and she had to stop herself from lusting over her son's fiancee. On the ride to Huntsville, Candy and Sonya made small talk. About an hour into the ride Drop called Candy's phone.

"What's up bay?" Candy answered the phone.

"Let me speak to my mama!"

"You're welcome too!" Candy said sarcastically then she handed Sonya the phone.

"Hello!"

"What's up Ma?"

"Not shit! What you done got into now Drop?"

"It's the same bullshit, but look I need you to handle shit for me. Call Carl Lee and tell him to bring you the trap phone and lace you up on game." Drop trusted his mama more than he trusted Carl

Lee. Even though he knew Carl Lee had been clean for close to a month, he still trusted Sonya more.

"Drop, give me a few days. I just got out and I ain't trying to jump into shit head first! So give me a few days." Sonya couldn't believe how Drop was trying to put a pack in her hands so fast.

"Aight! Give Candy the phone!" Drop said dryly sounding disappointed in Sonya's answer.

"Hello!" Candy got on the phone.

"Take her shopping for some clothes." Drop hung up the phone mad. Candy looked at the phone in disbelief that Drop had just hung up on her.

"I wouldn't take that shit from him if I was you. His disrespectful ass! Wants me to jump into the streets head first and I ain't been out an hour yet." Sonya couldn't believe how inconsiderate Drop was being. She felt like he was treating her like a dope fiend and it brought tears to her eyes. Candy looked over at Sonya and saw a tear rolling down her cheek while she fired up a cigarette.

"It's gonna be okay! We'll have some fun chilling together." Candy reached over and patted Sonya on her thigh.

"Girl, I ain't stuttin Drop! He always treats me badly. You see his sister didn't bother to come get me." Sonya wiped her eyes while she smoked. I would treat me like that too, thought Sonya as her mind drifted off.

Eleven years earlier..........

Slurp Slurp Slurp Slurp

"Ah yeah! Suck that dick, bitch! Daddy gonna give you a nice big rock!" Rocky told Sonya who was butt naked on her knees taking all of his dick in her mouth.

"You like that, Daddy?" Sonya stroked Rocky's dick with both of her hands while she talked nasty to him. She wanted Rocky to cum so she could get her smoke on. Sonya had been letting Rocky sell dope from her apartment just so she could get high for free.

"Yeah, just like that!" Sonya put Rocky's dick back into her mouth. Rocky felt himself about to explode, but then the front door came open and ten year old Drop and eleven year old Sweets came in the house from school. Sonya stopped and tried to raise up but Rocky grabbed her by her hair.

"Bitch, if you want this rock then you needs to keep sucking!" Sonya looked into her kids eyes then turned her head and went back to bobbin' on Rocky's dick. Sweets looked at her mama in disgust. She hated her mama and wished her daddy was out of prison.

"I can't wait til my daddy get out. I'ma tell him what you be doing for crack." Said Sweets.

"Shut up you lil bitch! You ain't gonna tell yo daddy shit!" Said Rocky. Then he stood up from the couch butt naked and slapped Sweets so hard in the face that she fell to the floor. Sweets started crying hysterically. Drop took off running to his bedroom.

"Why did you do that, Rocky?" Sonya sounded pitiful.

"Shut up bitch, and finish!" Rocky sat back down on the couch and Sonya went back to work sucking.

Drop climbed up to the top shelf in his closet and got the gun Carl Lee left him with before he went to prison. Drop walked back to the front room with the 38 revolver in his hands. he stood directly behind Sonya while she sucked Rocky's dick. Drop bit his bottom lip as he raised the gun with both hands pointing it directly at Rocky's chest. Rocky didn't see Drop because he had his head leaned back with his eyes closed, enjoying the pleasure of the head he was receiving.

Click Click Click

By the time Rocky opened his eyes and saw Drop standing behind Sonya with a pistol pointed at him it was too late.

Plow Click Click

The one bullet that was in the revolver ripped through Rocky's upper abdomen damn near hitting Sonya in the side of her face. Sonya jumped up screaming from the sight of all the blood. Drop grabbed Sweets by the arm pulling her up from the floor and they ran out of the apartment. When Sonya made it to the door, Drop and Sweets were riding away on their bikes.

The cigarette Sonya had between her fingers burnt her finger bringing her out of her day dream. I can't believe the shit that I used to do, thought Sonya as she plunked the cigarette butt out the window.

"Is there anywhere you need to go before we go shopping?" Candy asked Sonya when they reached Huntsville City limits.

"Nay, baby, I don't even wanna go shopping! All I want you to do is take me by Popeyes and take me to the house." Candy took Sonya by Popeyes and they went home. When they pulled up at Drop's condo, Sonya appreciated the fact that Drop stayed on the outskirts of the city.

"Home sweet home! That's your room, first door to the right. I bought you toiletries, a few outfits and under clothes from Victoria's Secret last week. You have your own bathroom. Make yourself at home, Mama." Candy sat down and started eating her food.

Sonya ate her food then went to take a bath. Sonya got into the tub and soaked in the bubble bath water for an hour. She thoroughly washed her body with scented body wash over and over again till she was satisfied that she no longer smelled like prison. Sonya got out of the tub and wrapped herself in a towel then she walked across the hall to her room. She stepped in front of the full body mirror, took the towel from around her and started drying off with it. Sonya admired her body as she looked at herself in the mirror while she dried her body. To be her age Sonya was sexy as hell. She turned backwards putting her back to the mirror and then she looked back into the mirror and made her thick thighs and fat ass shake. Sonya's mind floated back twenty-three years ago to the first night she danced at Fat Cats, a strip club in Huntsville, Alabama.

To all the ladies in the place
With style and grace,
Allow me to lace
These lyrical dishes in ya bushes

Biggie Smalls blasted from the speakers throughout the club as Sonya downed a double shot of straight Tequila. Sonya sat the shot glass down and walked to the stage looking edible in a pink two piece Calvin Klein bikini set. Her pretty face, thick thighs, plump breasts and juicy fat ass was making all the stripperss at work envious of Sonya. She climbed up on stage and walked up to the pole. Sonya put both hands around the pole, dropped down low and started making her nineteen year old ass pop in every direction.

Carl Lee walked in the club dressed in a Coogi sweatsuit looking like money. With his hair cut in a fresh temp Carl Lee's waves were deep as the ocean. His grill shined bright with four golds on top and four on the bottom. The Air Jordan cologne he had on made the women turn their heads to see where the fragrance was coming from.

Sonya saw Carl Lee walking to the bar while she was on the stage shaking her ass and she fell in love at first sight. She watched Carl Lee as he retrieved a bottle of Patron and a thousand singles from the bartender while he made small talk with the niggas and hoes who walked up to him, treating him like a celebrity. Damn he is so fine, thought Sonya as she watched Carl Lee leave the bar and walk toward her direction. Oh God, he's walking up to me, Sonya thought to herself.

Carl Lee stopped in front of Sonya, sat his bottle of Patron on the stage and then started throwing money on Sonya while she danced. After Carl Lee threw five hundred dollars on Sonya, he picked up his bottle and walked away from the stage, leaving Sonya intrigued about who he was. As soon as the song ended, Sonya got off the stage and made it her business to go find Carl Lee. Sonya spotted Carl Lee in the back of the club ducked off in a corner. She walked up to him.

"Thanks for the money!" Sonya said smiling.

"You welcome lil baby!" Carl Lee told Sonya and then he fired up the primo blunt he had between his lips.

"Can I hit that?" Carl lee looked at Sonya and knew that she didn't know any better.

"Nah baby girl! This that grown man shit right here, it's laced with hard rock." Carl Lee warned Sonya that the blunt had crack in it.

"I'm a big girl! I can handle it." Sonya took the blunt from Carl Lee's hand and put it to her lips.

"Miss Sweets!" Candy's voice snapped Sonya out of the day dream she was having. Sonya looked up and she saw Candy standing in the doorway looking at her.

"I'm sorry for intruding on you like that, but I heard you back here talking to someone and when I came to see who you were talking to, you were dancing." Candy had been watching Sonya for two minutes.

"I'm good baby! Pay me no mind!" Sonya walked over to the bed, grabbed her panties and put them on.

"For you to be a grandma, you got some moves on you, and your body is bangin'!" Candy complimented Sonya.

"Thanks child! God did look out for me by blessin' me with this pretty face and sexy body!" Sonya did a pose and they both burst into laughter. Candy went back to the front room and Sonya finished getting dressed while she thought about the first time she got high, on the first night she stripped, when she met Carl Lee for the first time.

****

Niece had been living from hotel room to hotel room every since Sweets had put her out. She was supposed to go to work in a few hours, but Jr. Jack the nigga she met at work last night was on his way up to her room to chill with her. When Jr. Jack fell up in the Player's Club last night, every bitch in the club flocked to him. His wavy hair, chocolate skin, gold teeth and big boy Gucci link gold chain had all the hoes trying to eat him. Just so happen Jr. Jack liked his women thick as hell and he was a fan of short hair, so Niece ended up being the one he hollered at to get her number before he left the club.

Niece got out of the shower and lotioned up in Angel body lotion from Victoria's Secrets. Smelling good enough to eat, Niece put on a pair of boyshorts and a halter. Then she laid back in the bed and smoked a blunt while she scrolled on facebook.

Ring Ring Ring

"Hello!" Niece answered her phone smiling when she saw Jr. Jack's name on the screen.

"Open the door!" Niece jumped out of bed and opened the door.

"What's up lil baby?" Jr. Jack stepped into the room wearing a True Religion outfit and some Deebo house shoes on his feet.

"You daddy! You know I been thinking about you since you left the club last night." Niece slung her ass from side to side as she walked to the bed. Jr. Jack couldn't help from grabbing his dick through his jeans. I'm about to slay this lil hoe, thought Jr. Jak as he sat on the bed next to Niece. Niece had been anticipating this moment for a few hours so she got straight to the point

"I wanna fuck, daddy!" Niece was horny and she was ready to freak Jr. Jack. With that said, Jr. Jack stood up and started stripping out of his clothes. Niece did the same. When she laid eyes on Jr. Jacks' rock hard pole, her pussy got wet instantly.

Let me give this bitch "The Test" before this shit goes any further, thought Jr. Jack, then he dug his finger into his ear. He took his finger out of his ear and saw he had ear wax on the end of his finger so he proceeded with "The Test." Niece was laid on her back, butt naked with her legs spread wide open exposing her pussy to the fullest. Jr. Jack reached between Nieces legs like he was about to just play with her pussy, but he stuck his finger that had the ear wax on it inside of Niece's pussy.

"Arrghhh!" Niece jumped up from the bed screaming. It felt like somebody had shot her pussy with a nail gun. Niece then went to the bathroom to piss. Jr. Jack knew Niece had a gangsta STD when she reacted the way she did from the ear wax. Niece didn't know what had happened but when she came from the bathroom Jr. Jack was getting dressed and shaking his head in disbelief at the same damn time.

"What's wrong? You leaving?" Niece was confused in more than one way.

"Lil baby, you gotta get ya pussy in check if you wanna fuck with ah nigga like me!"

"What you saying? I know I don't stank!" Niece shot back.

"Nah, but you need to go get that pussy treated cause you got something and you don't even know it!" Jr. Jack slid his feet into his DeeBo's and politely left out of Niece's room glad that he wasn't caught slippin in his pimpin.

Niece was lost but she knew Jr. Jack had to know what he was talking about because she had never felt the sharp pain that she felt when he stuck his finger inside of her pussy. She grabbed a sweat suit from her suitcase and threw it on with some Nike Foamposites. Niece left the hotel and went to Crestwood Hospital. There was only a few people in the emergency room area so she only had to wait thirty minutes before she was seen by the nurse. Niece explained her situation to the nurse once they were in the back. The nurse made Niece urinate in a cup then the nurse swabbed Niece's vagina with a long Q-Tip. Twenty minutes later the doctor came in and told Niece she had an STD but they wouldn't know exactly what it was until the results came back from the lab. To top it off, he told Niece she was pregnant. Niece's heart sunk into her big toe and she started crying. The doctor left and came back with a small paper cup containing four pills inside it. He gave the cup to Niece and told her to take the pills. After she took the pills, the doctor gave her a shot of penicillin in her ass.

Niece cried as she drove back to the hotel. She thought about how her life had taken a dramatic turn since she started working at the Player's Club. She hadn't talked to her mom in damn near a month, since she stopped going to school. Every time Niece's mom calle her, Niece would tell her mama that she was busy studying or giving her any type of bogus ass lie just to get off the phone with her. Now her mama was the only person she wanted to talk to.

****

Drop was sitting in the dayroom area of the block watching the nine o'clock news when Po Boy came into the block. Po Boy was from Drop's side of town and he was a known D-boy throughout the city of Hunts Vegas. Po Boy and Drop had done business together on several occasions. Po Boy went to sit his mat on his rack and make up his bunk. By the time he finished Drop walked up on him.

"What's up my boy?" Po Boy looked up and saw it was Drop hollerin at him.

"Shit! What's up my boy?" They dapped each other up.

"Mane sweating those bitch narcs to take this hold off ah nigga so I can bail. Drop knew they couldn't hold him too much longer without giving him a bond.

"My boy don't you know them fuck boys Craigs and Wilson pulled me over and planted some work in my box chevy." Drop was astounded by what he was hearing.

"Them bitch niggas did the exact same thing to me, my boy!" Po Boy wasn't surprised.

"I heard somebody lit up that fuck nigga Fat Rabbit last night at the La Quinta on University cross from Olive garden. The folks don't know who did it cause the surveillance cameras at the hotel don't work. They say that fat bitch in a coma or on life support or somethin." Po Boy's words were music to Drop's ears.

"Oh yeah! Damn! I wish I could've got to that fat fuck first!" Drop was mad that he hadn't killed Fat Rabbit.

"His baby mama nem talkin bout as soon as they find out who did it, they gonna press charges and shit!" Po Boy gave Drop more details about Fat Rabbit. They talked for another ten minutes then Drop went to use the phone. A midst of sweat formed on Drop's forehead as he listened to the phone ring. He didn't know if he was anxious or if anxiety was setting in.

"You have a collect call from "Drop" an inmate at the

Huntsville Metro Jail. Press one to accept." Was all the recording got to say before Candy accepted the call.

"Hey bay! Are you still mad at me?" Candy was happy that Drop had called. She hadn't talked to him in hours.

"That doesn't matter right now. I want you to listen to me and listen to me good. Candice, do you hear me?" Candy knew Drop was serious when he called her by her real name.

"Yeah baby. I hear you!" Candy started tearing up cause she didn't know what Drop was about to say next.

"I need you to go finish that date you went on last night!" Drop couldn't say what he really wanted to say so he needed for Candy to read between the lines. The phone went silent while Candy thought about what Drop was telling her.

"Okay baby, I got you Ivan!" Candy knew what she needed to do.

"Okay baby, I'll call you tomorrow." Drop knew that Candy had read between the lines.

"I love you bay!" Candy missed Drop.

"I love you most!" Drop hung up the phone with Candy and called Carl Lee. Drop told Carl Lee to go pick up Sonya early in the morning, give her the trap phone and take her to get a rental car. Carl Lee was glad that he didn't have to run the show anymore because all the communicating with crackheads had him about ready to get high again.

Candy called Sweets when she got off the phone with Drop. Sweets gave Candy all the info she knew on Fat Rabbit's whereabouts and condition. When they got off the phone, Candy thought about the fact that Sweets didn't ask about Sonya. Damn that's crazy, thought Candy then she started putting her plan together to finish her date from the previous night.

CHAPTER 9

The next morning Sonya woke up with a lot on her mind. She decided that she was gonna be there for Drop like he asked her to. If he trust me enough to handle his business for him, then I must be capable of doing it without fucking up, thought Sonya as she sat on the edge of the bed and fired up a cigarette. Images of Lay Lay popped into Sonya's head and she realized that she hadn't talked to Lay Lay since she had got out. Then Sonya's mind went to her daughter Sweets, who she hadn't talked to in over three years. Sonya wanted a relationship with her child, but Sweets was one tough cookie. Sweets was stubborn and stuck in her ways, just like her mama.

"Baby mama, baby mama, I'm tired of you! It's to the point that I wanna fire you. You play the games like a child would do!" Sonya thought she was trippin when she heard a familiar voice singing Lil Boosie's first hit song. Sonya walked to the front room where she was met by Carl Lee with open arms. Candy couldn't do nothing but smile as she watched the two reunite.

"Damn bay! You got out yesterday and didn't even call ah nigga!" Carl Lee told Sonya as he held her. Then he took a step back to get a good look at Sonya. With that good look at her, he fell in love all over again.

"Boy, why you looking at me like that?" Sonya laughed.

"Got damn, baby, you fine as wine baby! Let baby daddy taste them sweet juices!" Carl Lee licked his lips.

"Boy stop! And what are you doing over here so early!" Sonya had love for Carl Lee but she didn't fuck with him for real because a small piece of her always told her that Carl Lee was the reason for all the bullshit that she had done and been through, but Sonya knew deep down inside that she couldn't blame no one but herself for her actions.

"Ya son told me to come get you this morning, give you this phone and take you to the spot to show you where everything at." Carl Lee handed Sonya the trap phone. You can handle it Sonya, thought Sonya as she looked at the phone.

"Let me get myself together then!" Sonya walked off to her room.

"Can I watch?" Carl Lee followed behind Sonya. When Carl Lee and Sonya left the condo, Carl Lee took Sonya by Cal Mae's house for a second then he took her to the stash spot where Drop kept his dope at. Sonya was shocked that the stash spot was a nice four bedroom, two bathroom house that Drop had purchased on Skyline Circle off of Sparkman Drive. The inside of the house looked like someone lived in it, having nice furniture and HD TV's mounted on the walls. Carl Lee took Sonya to the basement level of the house where the safe was at.

"Push three-zero-zero-one and unlock!" Carl Lee demonstrated and the safe door automatically slowly swung open. Sonya's stomach started turning flips and she farted when she saw all the crack that was inside the safe.

"Damn girl, you stank! You sure you gonna be able to handle this shit? I know a dope fart when I smell one." Carl Lee knew Sonya was gonna have to be strong in order not to get high. Sonya looked at Carl Lee.

"Yeah! I'm straight!"

Ring Ring Ring

Sonya jumped from the phone ringing. When she looked at the phone, she saw that it was Lay Lay calling.

"Please talk to your lil girlfriend. She's been calling since you left the damn prison. That's how I knew ya ass was out. I tried to get her to play in that pussy for me last night but she wouldn't do it." Carl Lee saw that it was Lay Lay calling.

"Hey baby!" Sonya answered.

"Why ain't you called me, Sonya? You just done said fuck me already! And I thought you said this was your son's number. The nigga said he ya damn baby daddy." Lay Lay ranted on not giving Sonya a chance to say anything.

"Baby look, there is a lot goin on. My son in jail and I'm trying to get him out as we speak. Answer the phone at one thirty, okay! I____" Sonya knew Lay Lay was pissed because Lay Lay hung up on her.

"You sucked on that lil baby's pussy and made her fall in love with yo stankin ass, just like you done me." Carl Lee said smiling from ear to ear.

"Boy shut the fuck up!" Sonya twisted her lips.

"It ain't my fault you know how to suck a beach ball through a hose pipe. Come on, let's go get somethin to eat." Carl Lee took Sonya to Betty Mae's Soul Food where they ate. Sonya had fried pork chops, fried corn, fried okra and pinto beans. Carl Lee ate fried chicken, baked macaroni and cheese, black eyed peas and hot water bread. After they ate, Carl Lee took Sonya to Avis car rental where she drove away in a new Impala. She had several bubs waiting on her to come serve them.

****

Fat Rabbit's baby mama and his sister came out of his hospital room and walked right past Candy who was in full disguise, wearing an old fashioned wig on her head, a scrub outfit and a name badge that she stole from a medical student who was in the employee break room. Candy heard them discussing where they were about to go eat at then she watched them get on the elevator. Showtime, thought Candy as she walked to Fat Rabbit's room. Candy's palms started sweating as she looked at Fat Rabbit laying in the hospital bed completely unconscious with IVs running into his arms, mouth and nose. "You can do it!" Candy hyped herself up as she walked up closer to the bed and found the IV that provided Fat Rabbit with oxygen. Candy slid on a pair of gloves then she clamped the oxygen IV. Candy walked out of the room. She heard the heart monitor flatline as soon as she stepped into the hallway. When she turned the corner, nurses ran past her going to Fat Rabbit's room. Candy started feeling sick in the stomach while she waited for the elevator to open.

Ding

The elevator opened and Candy got inside. She was ready to get the hell out of the hospital. When the elevator opened for her to get off, there was five people getting onto the elevator. Candy thought they were about to detain her. She hurried past them without making any eye contact with anyone. As soon as she reached the outside of the hospital she vomited. Candy got herself together and ran to her car. I can't believe I just killed somebody, thought Candy as she drove home. When she made it inside the condo, Candy ran to the bathroom where she stripped out of her clothes and jumped into the shower. She felt filthy from head to toe. Candy scrubbed her body for thirty minutes straight. Then she got out of the shower, wrapped up with a towel and went and laid in the bed. Candy smiled at the thought of her being down for her man. I can't wait for Drop to call, thought Candy as she closed her eyes to go to sleep. She didn't know why she felt so tired.

****

Sweets had been chilling lately, spending a lot of time with her son. She was tired of the life she had been living over the course of the past few years. Last week she registered to take some college courses at Virginia College. Sweets even found a few buildings that she could turn into salons. She was ready to boss up for her twenty-fourth birthday and leave that strip club shit behind her.

"Mama, mama I won some more tickets!" Bud Bud ran up to Sweets holding the tickets he'd won.

"That's good baby! Put 'em up here and go win us some more!" Sweets smiled as she watched her son run off to go play. She thought about how when she was a lil girl her mom never took her and Drop anywhere. The only place her mama took them was over to one of her dope smoking buddies house or dropped them off at Cal Mae's house without a change of clothes. Cal Mae always took Drop and Sweets shopping for the newest clothes whenever Sonya dropped them off and wouldn't come back to get them for days sometimes weeks. The eight years Carl Lee was in prison was the roughest years of Sweet's life.

"Excuse me, beautiful, but I would be less of a man if I didn't tell you how beautiful you are." A male voice interrupted Sweets thoughts and the smell of Gentlemen Only by Givenchy filled her nostrils. When Sweets turned her head to the right, she starred in the face of the fine-specimen that was talking to her. Damn, he's cute, thought Sweets as she admired the guy's clear eyes, dreadlocks, light brown skin and pretty white teeth. Sweets could tell by the guy's appearance that he was drug free.

"Thanks and you're handsome yourself." Sweets told him.

"My name is Thomas!" He reached out his hand to shake

Sweet's hand.

"Mama, mama look!" Bud Bud ran up to Sweets.

"That's good baby! Go win us some more!" Sweets grabbed the tickets from Bud Bud and he ran off.

"I'm Sweets!" She shook Thomas's hand.

"That must be your lil man right there, huh!" Thomas pointed at Bud Bud.

"Yep! That's my man. So Thomas, what brings you to Chucky Cheese?" Sweets was curious.

"It's my daughter's birthday!" Thomas pointed to a group of kids on the other side of the room. Sweets saw a lil girl wearing a crown so she figured that must be his daughter.

"Oh, she's pretty! Don't get in trouble over here trying to talk to me." Sweets said sarcastically.

"Nah, Sweetie, my BM's boyfriend is here. We just co-parent. I live in Decatur. Thomas assured Sweets that it was nothing between him and his baby mama. They talked a few more minutes and exchanged phone numbers promising each other they were gonna call one another.

****

"Kira, get up!" Screamed Shelley as she shook Kira to wake her up. Kira opened her eyes to see what Shelley wanted. They had become best friends, lovers and JB's hoes. They all still lived at the King's Inn hotel together, smoking crack on a daily basis.

"What Shelley?" Kira rolled over out of her sleep to find JB on the floor shaking with white shit foaming from his mouth and a needle stuck in his arm. Kira jumped up from the bed in panic mode. "Oh shit! What happened Shelley?" Kira was scared as hell.

"I don't know! Hell, I was sleep when I heard a loud thump. When I woke up I seen him like this and I woke you up." Kira called the ambulance and they arrived in less than five minutes. The ambulance wouldn't let Kira nor Shelley ride in the ambulance with JB because they weren't family. They got in Kira's car to go to the hospital but it wouldn't start up. For ten minutes they tried to crank the car.

"Shid girl, it's hot! Let's go back in the room. They said he'll be alright anyway." Shelley knew that JB had started fuckin with heroin.

"Yeah, you right! Come on, let's get something to smoke. Call ol' boy!" Kira got out the car. Her and Shelley went back into the room.

"What you wanna get?" Shelley counted her money.

"Get a quarter so we'll be straight for a while." Kira said as she straightened up the mess in he room.

Ring Ring Ring

"Yeah!" Sonya answered the phone as she pulled into the driveway of the stash house to get some work.

"Hey, where Carl Lee or Drop at?" Said Shelley.

"Everything all ball! What you want and where you at?" Sonya hadn't been serving for a full two hours and she was already in the swing of thangs as if she hadn't been gone away for three years.

"Oh, okay! This Shelley, I'm at the Kings Inn room 218. Can you bring me a quack?" Shelley figured that the woman on the phone was Drop's mama cause Carl Lee had said she was getting out soon.

"I'll be there in twenty minutes!" Sonya hung up as she walked into the stash house. She grabbed the work she needed to go catch her plays and then she left. Sonya smiled as she drove away from the stash house because she noticed that she hadn't thought about smoking any dope. That shit is a thing of my past, thought Sonya as she turned up Future's song "Might as well" on the radio. When she made it to the King's Inn, she called Shelley's phone.

"Hello!" Shelley answered

"Open the door!" Sonya was stepping out of the car. She knew to never do business on the outside of a hotel or motel. That was a for sure way to catch a case and go to jail. Shelley opened the door and Sonya walked in.

"Dang! Carl Lee said you were beautiful!" Shelley couldn't believe how pretty Sonya was.

"Thanks! Here!" Sonya handed Shelley the dope and Shelley gave her the money. Kira came walking out of the bathroom with a towel wrapped around her wet body. Sonya thought her mind was playing tricks on her, but there was no way that this was Lay Lay standing in front of her. Who the fuck is this lil pretty bitch right here, thought Sonya as her lesbian instincts kicked in.

"Who is she, Shelley?" Kira saw the way Sonya was looking at her.

"I'm Sonya, and who are you, beautiful?" Sonya didn't need anybody to talk for her.

"Oh, okay! I'm Kira!" Kira blushed. How small would the world be if she was Lay Lay's twin sister. That's crazy. Ain't no way in the hell she's smoking crack, thought Sonya as she raped Kira with her eyes

"You can chill with us if you want to!" Shelley saw how Sonya was molesting Kira with her eyes, plus Shelley knew Sonya use to smoke.

"Nah, I think I'm about to go!" Sonya's mind was telling her to leave as she watched Shelley fire up her pipe, but the freak inside of her was telling her to stay when she put her eyes on Kira.

"You're pretty as hell and thick too!" Said Kira as she took the pipe from Shelley and fired up. Damn, that lil baby smoking yams, thought Sonya as she watched Kira blow out crack smoke. Kira handed Shelley the pipe the she dropped the towel she had on and started lotioning up. The way Sonya's eyes bucked from her head you would've thought she hit the pipe. Her eyes were glued to Kira's pretty and freshly shaved pussy. Sonya watched Kira's every movement as she lotioned her body. This bitch wants Kira bad, thought Shelley.

"Kira gone lay down and let her see that pussy!" Shelley teased.

"She don't wanna see this pussy, do you?" Kira giggled then she laid down on the bed. Kira spread her thighs and exposed all of her pretty pussy to Sonya. Even though Kira had lost about fifteen pounds, she was still fine as hell. Sonya's mouth got wetter than the Tennessee River as she watched Kira part her pussy lips to allow Sonya to see her clit. Sonya wasn't aware of her actions. The only thing she knew was that she was in the bed only inches away from Kira's pretty pussy.

Lick Lick Lick Lick

"Ooh shit! Sexy damn!" Kira moaned from the pleasure of Sonya's tongue flicking across her clit. Sonya zoned out on Kira and had a feast. Kira grabbed Sonya's head while she received some of the best head in America.

"Ahh, ahh, yes! I'm bout to cum!" Kira couldn't believe that she was about to climax so fast. Sonya started sucking on Kira's clit, sending Kira to neva neva land.

"Hmm, hmm, ahh!" Kira's whole body shook. Shelley watched in amazement.

"Damn she's good!" Said Shelley then she fired up her pipe. Sonya raised up and looked Kira in the eyes. They shared a psychosexual moment.

"Muah!" Sonya blew Kira a kiss. Kira felt the kiss in her heart. Sonya began walking out of the room. She wanted to stay but she couldn't tolerate the crack smoke. Kira jumped up from the bed and caught Sonya at the door.

"Don't leave me, beautiful! I mean I feel like there is something between us more special than just you eating my pussy.' Kira didn't know what had come over her, but she did know her words were true. She gets easily sprung just like her twin, thought Sonya.

"Baby if you really mean what you say, then you would have to stop smokin that shit!" Sonya wasn't about to be fucking with no bitch who smokin. That might cause her to relapse. Kira stood speechless. Sonya leaned forward and kissed Kira on her forehead. Then she walked out of the room and got in the car. It would be nice to have a set of sexy twins in love with me at the same time, thought Sonya as she pulled off smiling.

Kira went to the bathroom to wash up after Sonya left. She couldn't believe that she was actually feeling some type of way about a woman. Kira looked in the mirror and became disgusted with herself and her current situation. Tears began running down her face. It ain't meant for me to be living like this. That's why God got JB away so I can get away, thought Kira and she walked into the room.

"Girl, she made your pussy cum in thirty seconds flat!" Shelley said, laughing. Then she hit her pipe. Kira was tired of her trashy ass too.

"What's her number?" Kira asked Shelley who had a mouth full of smoke.

"Oh, somebody wants some more of that good head. It's

652-1111." Shelley said after she exhaled the crack smoke from her mouth. Kira picked up her phone and called Sonya. She had to get away from Shelley and everything else.

"Yeah, who dis?" Sonya answered.

"This is Kira, the girl you just left. Are you far from here?"

"Nah lil baby, I'm just around the block, but what's up?"

"Can you please come back to get me?" I don't wanna be here anymore." Sonya smiled at Kira's request.

"I'm on my way!" Sonya did a u-turn on the Parkway and went back to the hotel. Shelley watched Kira pack her belongings into her suitcase. Kira then walked over to Shelley and gave her a hug.

"Be good, Kira!" Shelley was tearing up.

"I will Shelley. You do the same!"

Knock Knock Knock

Kira released Shelley and went and opened the door. Sonya was smiling when the door opened.

"You ready baby!"

"Yeah, I'm ready!" Kira grabbed her stuff and left the room with Sonya. I'll just have to send a wrecker to get my car, thought Kira as they pulled away from the hotel.

****

"Lamont Walker died today at the Huntsville Hospital where

he'd been in a coma for the past two days after he was shot two nights ago at the LaQuinta Inn on University. Up next is sports with Rickey Wilkerson." Said the newscaster as Drop and Po Boy watched the five o'clock news. A smile spread across Drop's face. Good job baby, thought Drop.

"Inmate Ivan Sweets ATW!" The CO announced over the intercom.

"That's you ain't it, my boy?" Said Po Boy.

"Hell yeah, my boy! I'm up out dis bitch! Hit me up as soon as you get out!" Drop went to grab his mattress. An officer came to the pod to get Drop and walked him to the elevator. Drop knew he was being taken to booking. Damn, it's about time, thought Drop. When they made it to the booking room, Drop saw his property sitting on the table next to the officer sitting behind the computer.

"Get your bag and go get dressed in that room!" The officer pointed to the room where Drop was to get dressed in. When Drop came out of the room, the same narcotics that pulled him over and planted the dope in his car was there waiting for him.

"It's not everyday that we run into one of you lil punk ass drug dealers who is solid" Craigs told Drop.

"Yeah I knew for sure he was gonna use the card we gave him!" Wilson commented as Drop opened the door to walk into the lobby where his lawyer and Carl Lee was at waiting for him.

"I was gonna use your card but you forgot to put your mama number on it!"

"Muthafucka I'll___!" Wilson reached for Drop.

"Chill out Wilson!" Craigs grabbed Wilson.

"Ivan are you okay or do I need to file harassment charges on these gentlemen?" Asked Mr. White, Drop's lawyer.

"Nah, I'm good, let's go!" Drop smiled at the Narcs.

"Come by my office or call me if you have any problems!"

"I will!"

"You good baby?" Carl Lee asked Drop as soon as they stepped foot outside the precinct.

"Yeah, I'm good! Just get me to the crib!" Drop fired up a Newport as he got into Carl Lee's Lumina. They watched their mirrors to make sure they weren't being followed as they drove to Drop's condo. Carl Lee started smilin when they pulled up and he seen Sonya's rental car.

"Why you smiling and shit nigga? You happy or somethin? Got damn Sonya do all that to you!" Drop picked with Carl Lee.

"Nigga, that's that baby right there." Carl Lee admitted.

Drop and Carl Lee were taken by surprise when they entered the house and saw Sonya and Kira sitting at the kitchen table eating. This bitch trippin, thought Carl Lee when he saw Sonya with the same fiend that he watched get beat up at the room where Shelley was at.

"Hey son!" Sonya got up from the table and went and hugged Drop. Drop was happy to see Sonya, but he had no idea who the fuck she had in his house.

"Who dat?" Drop whispered in Sonya's ear as they hugged. Kira had lost so much weight that Drop didn't recognize her.

"That's my new girl!" Drop shook his head and walked to his bedroom where he found Candy in the bed knocked out. Drop walked over to Candy, leaned down, and kissed her on her lips.

"I love you!" Drop told her in her ear. Candy opened her eyes jumped up and punched Drop in the face.

"Who are you and what are you trying to do to me?" Candy screamed. Drop didn't know what the hell was going on.

"Baby what are you talking about? It's me baby, Drop!" Drop tried to grab Candy but she grabbed the lamp off of the night stand and threw it at him.

"Stay the fuck away from me!" Candy screamed. Sonya, Kira and Carl Lee heard the commotion so they ran to Drop's room.

"Baby, chill out!" Drop saw that something was seriously wrong by the look in Candy's eyes. Drop reached for her again, but she screamed.

"Don't fucking touch me!" Candy was acting like a cat that was backed into a corner.

"Candy, what's wrong friend!" Kira couldn't believe how Candy was acting. Everybody looked at Kira like "Who the fuck are you?" but Candy knew exactly who she was.

"Kira, what are they trying to do to me?" Cried Candy. Drop couldn't believe how much Kira's appearance had changed.

"Kira can you talk to her?" Drop pleaded.

"Come to me Candy. Nobody is gonna hurt you." Kira walked up closer to the bed and reached her arm out for Candy to grab hold to.

"You promise, Kira?" Candy wanted to make sure Kira wasn't lying.

"I swear to you Candy!" Kira finally had Candy convinced that nobody was gonna hurt her. Candy grabbed Kira's arm and stepped off of the bed.

"Kira, get her dressed so we can take her to the hospital. Come on y'all!" Drop motioned for Sonya and Carl Lee to follow him to the front while Kira got Candy dressed.

"Mane what the fuck is you thinking about bringing that crackhead over here?" Carl Lee blurted out loud at Sonya. Drop looked confused.

"She said she doesn't wanna fuck around anymore, plus she's my bitch now. So stay the fuck out of my business." Sonya was getting pissed.

"So what you gonna do when Lay Lay get out in two weeks, huh. Don't worry, I'll take good care of her cause by then ya ass gonna be back smoking if you fuckin with that lil hoe in there." Carl Lee fired up a cigarette. Kira heard everything that had been said. Nothing hurt accept the fact that she heard her twin sister's name and she knew it was her twin because she was getting out in two weeks.

"Boy, shut the fuck up and get out my business!" Sonya was mad as hell at Carl Lee.

"Well I'm fuckin glad she was here cause she's the only person Candy knew out of all of us. Drive any one of those cars you wanna drive, I'm bout to drive yo rental to take Candy to the hospital." Drop went to the bedroom and got Kira and Candy then left out the house.

"What the fuck you waiting on to leave?" Sonya asked Carl Lee.

"That's okay bitch., When you start back smoking don't come back to me trying to suck this dick for a crumb." Carl Lee hit Sonya with a low blow then walked out of the house.

"Aghh I can't stand his bitch ass!" Sonya screamed. Drop, Candy and Kira sat inside the emergency room waiting to be seen by the doctor. Drop was trippin on how Candy really didn't know who he was. Damn she done lost some weight, thought Drop when he looked at Kira, who looked like she had been smoking dope. After they sat for an hour, the doctor came out and took Candy to the back. Drop dropped his head into his hands as he thought about all the things that could possibly be wrong with Candy.

"It's gonna be okay, Ivan!" Drop raised his head when Kira said his real name.

"How you know my name?"

"Your mom told me her son name was Ivan, that's why I didn't know who she was talking about till I seen you walk through the door."

"Awe, I didn't know who the fuck you was!"

"I've lost a few pounds, but you better believe a bitch bout to bounce back." Kira winked at Drop. She might have dropped a few pounds but she still prettier than ah muthafucka thought Drop. They sat in silence for the rest of the time that they waited for the doctor to let them know something. An hour later the doctor came out.

"Tell me something good doc!" Said Kira.

"Oh yes, everything will be fine with Candice. Over the course of the next few weeks or so, all of her memory will restore in full. She's suffering from a Psychotic Stenosis. Something dramatic happened to her then she went to sleep thinking about it heavily. By her doing so, her brain went into immediate anxiety and bruised her short term memory. I have to prescribe her some heavy meds, therefore she will need someone to stay by her side to assist her for a few weeks at the most." The doctor explained and Drop knew exactly why Candy was acting the way she was acting.

"Do y'all have somebody that can watch her around the clock for the next week or two?" The doctor looked at Kira then to Drop.

"Yes, I'll watch her around the clock , sir!" Kira said before Drop could say anything.

"Good! I'll write her prescription then yall can be on yalls way home." The doctor walked off.

"Kira, are you sure you don't mind staying at my house with Candy all day every day till she gets better?" Drop had to make sure Kira knew the responsibility she was taking on.

"Of course I don't mind. I need you to help me get my weight back up anyways. You will feed me, won't you?" Kira said sarcastically, causing Drop to laugh.

"Yeah, I got you lil mama!" I like her personality, thought Drop. Moments later the nurse walked Candy out and handed Drop her prescription. They left out the hospital.

"Aye, bitch Where you going ?" Drop, Candy and Kira turned around to see who was behind them talking crazy. Oh shit! Thought Kira when she saw JB running up on her.

"So bitch, you gonna act like you didn't hear me!" JB grabbed Kira by her hair. This nigga must be crazy, thought Drop.

"Aghhh! Please stop! No JB!" was all Drop had to hear to send him into action

BING BING BING

Drop hit JB with a three piece combo to his face that caused him to let go of Kira and fall to the ground. Drop went to the foot game.

DOOM DOOM DOOM

"Pussy ass nigga!" Said Drop as he stomped out JB who was on the ground balled up.

"I outta kill you bitch nigga!"

BOOM!

Drop kicked JB in his face one last time.

"Come on Kira, let's go!" Drop grabbed Candy who had no idea about anything that was happening right in front of her. JB laid on the ground leaking. Drop had really beat the shit out of him.

"Kira, stop crying! What are you crying for?" Candy asked Kira while they sat in the drive through window of Walgreens waiting on Candy's prescription.

"I'm good!" Kira said through sniffs. Drop grabbed the prescription and pulled off.

"Ya'll hungry?" Candy's meds specified that she eat before she takes the meds.

"Yeah, I am, but what's your name?" Candy had already asked Drop the same question fifty times.

"Drop!" He told her. Minutes later he pulled in the drive through of Schlotzsky's Deli and ordered everyone something to eat then drove home.

"Where are your clothes and stuff, Kira?" Drop asked Kira when he pulled up in front of the condo.

"I wonder why Antonio hasn't called me?" Candy blurted out. Drop looked at Candy then he turned to Kira. Kira shrugged her shoulders. Bitch you better shut the fuck up, thought Kira.

"They're in the trunk, Drop." Kira got out the car.

"Damn! So you and Sonya serious!" Drop laughed. Kira felt a little shame at the moment knowing that at one time she could have had Drop. Now she's a soon to be recovering dope fiend who talks to his mom who thinks she's gonna be fuckin twin sisters at the same time.

"She said if I wanted to better my situation then I should call her, so I did!" Kira told Drop as they walked into the condo. She didn't want Drop to think she was gone over Sonya. Who in the fuck is Antonio, thought Drop as he walked back to the car to get Kira's bags out the trunk. When he made it back the girls were eating so he went and showered. When he got out the shower he put on some gym shorts and a wife beater, then he went to the front. Kira was handing Candy a pill to take. Ten minutes later Candy fell asleep on the couch. Drop picked her up and carried her to the bed. Then he went back to the front where Kira was at looking uncomfortable.

"You make yourself at home. Even if you and Sonya don't work out this is still your home cause I fucks with you." Drops words put a smile on Kira's face.

"Thanks Ivan!" Kira said smiling.

"You welcome!" Drop grinned then turned on the PS4 to play 2K Basketball. Kira did like Drop told her to and she made herself at home. She took a good long shower and got dressed in some sweat pants and sat on the couch where she ended up falling asleep while she watched Drop play the game. Sonya came home around eleven that night. She was shocked to see Kira stretched out on the couch asleep.

"I see she made herself at home!" Sonya told Drop who was still playing the game.

"Yeah. I told her to. She gotta watch Candy for the next week or two anyways." Drop kept playing the game. Sonya was tired from all the ripping and running she had been doing so she went to her room and went to sleep.

CHAPTER 10

Sweets and Thomas had spent a lot of time on the phone since they first met yesterday at Chucky Cheese. Thomas had even managed to persuade Sweets to go on a date with him tonight. Sweets was ready for her date, but she had a problem. Her regular babysitter wasn't answering the phone. Damn, thought Sweets as she hung up her cell phone, mad that she didn't get an answer. Sweets only had one other option and that was to call Drop because she wasn't about to let her child go over to Cal Mae's house tonight. Sweets knew her grandma was holding her famous Tunk game tonight and if a muthafucka got wrong with Cal Mae her house could turn into Desert Storm with the quickness. Sweets made a mistake and called Drop's trap phone instead of his regular phone.

"Hello!" Sonya answered the phone. She was sitting on the couch with Kira watching TV.

"Where Drop at?" Sweets didn't have any words for Sonya.

"He's right here." Sonya heard the hate in Sweets voice. Drop walked from the kitchen to the den area.

"Well give him the phone!" Sweets was tired of hearing Sonya's voice. Sonya searched for something to say, but nothing came to her brain, so she handed Drop the phone.

"Who dis?" Drop asked Sonya. When Sonya tried to say something, she just fell to the floor crying.

"Why does my child hate me? God I'm sorry! I just want my baby to forgive me!" Drop knew exactly who was on the phone from what Sonya was crying.

"Sis!" Drop said into the phone as he looked at Sonya crying hysterically on the floor.

"Yeah bruh!" Sweets had her face twisted in disgust with Sonya.

"Mane, what did you say to her?" Drop seen Sonya was hurt but he also knew the reason behind the hurt.

"Bruh on some real shit, fuck that bitch! They could've kept that hoe in prison for all I give ah fuck. That hoe ain't never did shit for me!" Sweets meant every syllable of what she said and Drop felt where she was coming from.

"It is what it is, but what's up?" Drop said no longer caring about Sonya crying. Sonya could hear everything Sweets said anyways.

"I needed you to watch Bud Bud for me, but I don't want my child around that hoe!" Sweets hated Sonya's guts. Sonya got up from the floor, grabbed the keys to her rental and left out the door. Kira walked to the patio door and saw that Sonya was about to pull off. Drop couldn't help himself from looking at Kira's ass that was jiggling out of the boy shorts she was wearing just for him, but he didn't know that.

"Drop! Drop!" Sweets yelled in the phone when she didn't hear anything.

"Yeah, yeah, my bad! Sonya left so bring me my nephew." Drop told Sweets while he gawked at Kira's ass and gripped his dick through his gym shorts.

"Ok, bruh. Love you! Thanks! I'm on my way!" Sweets hung up the phone and got ready to leave.

Drop hadn't had any pussy in about a week and now Kira was looking like the same girl he met at the Player's Club. Kira could see Drop through the reflection of the patio door staring at her. Kira watched Drop grip his dick while he stared at her ass. She started making her ass shake. Drop slouched down on the couch and put his hand inside his shorts. Damn, I wanna fuck this bitch, thought Drop as he began stroking his dick. That dick long and thick too, thought Kira as she looked at Drop's dick standing up in his shorts. Kira turned around and walked up to Drop. Drop pulled on his dick extra hard when the print of Kira's fat pussy was dead in front of him. Kira got down on her knees.

"I'm gonna help you with your big problem, but we are not gonna fuck!" Kira pulled Drop's shorts down and moved his hand away from his dick. Then she put both of her hands around Drop's dick.

Spooh Spooh

Kira spit on Drop's dick twice getting it extra wet. Drop's

heart rate sped up from the attention he was receiving. The way Kira held his hard dick with a firm grip was driving him crazy.

He looked Kira in the eyes as she began stroking his dick. Kira put one of her hands around the base of Drop's dick and pulled down on it, making Drop's dick extend to the maximum. Then she started stroking the head of his dick with her other hand. Drop was gone over the way Kira was handling his dick. His dick started pulsating instantly.

"Hm, hm, hm, ahh!" Drop breathed like an animal as he nutted all over Kira's hands. Kira milked his dick like she was milking a cow, till nothing else came out of it. Drop and Kira stared deeply into one another's eyes for what seemed to be an eternity, but it was only a brief moment.

"Don't move! Let me get you a rag!" Kira got up to go to the bathroom.

"Kira, I'm hungry!" Kira damn near jumped out of her skin when Candy said her name as she walked out of the bedroom.

"Ooh shit, girl. You scared me!" Kira grabbed her chest. Drop looked over the couch he was sitting on and saw Candy in the hallway talking to Kira. He hurried and pulled his shorts up.

"Where's dude at Kira?" Candy was talking about Drop.

"He's right there on the couch! Kira pointed to where Drop was sitting. Candy walked over to Drop and took a good look at him.

"Didn't we go to the movies together and you got shot or something?" Candy's memory was trying to replenish. Drop smiled.

"Yeah baby! We went to the movies and I got shot!" Drop was glad to see that Candy's memory was coming back.

"I thought so! Drip, ain't that your name? Drip?'

"Nah baby, it's Drop!"

"Oh, okay!" Candy giggled then she walked to the kitchen where Kira was at warming up her food. Kira sat Candy's food on the table and Candy sat down to eat.

"Thanks girl! You got somethin on your shirt." Kira went into her room.

Knock Knock Knock

Drop got up to answer the door. He looked through the peephole and saw his sister holding his nephew. When Drop opened the door, he was surprised to find Sweets dressed in casual attire. Sweets was in a hurry so she carried Bud Bud to the couch, laid him down and left.

Candy took her medication right after she ate, then she went to the bedroom and went to sleep. Kira cleaned up the kitchen and then she took a shower. Drop sat on the couch fighting the temptation to go join Kira in the shower. Ten minutes after Drop heard the shower cut off, Kira sat down next to him on the couch wearing some sweat pants and a wife beater. Damn, she smells good, thought Drop as he inhaled the smell of the strawberry body wash Kira had showered in. Kira pulled Drop's chain out of her pocket.

"I think this belongs to you!" Kira held the chain out to

Drop. When he looked at the chain he smiled.

"How did you get this, I mean!" Drop was confuse, but Kira took the time to explain the whole story to him starting from the night she met him at the Player's Club. Drop was awestruck as he listened to Kira. The things she had been through and experienced in the last month alone was more than most people go through in a lifetime.

"Kira, through all that you've just told me, you still managed to keep my chain. I'm shocked. Shid, what do ah nigga owe you?" Drop couldn't believe that Kira was actually smoking crack and still didn't get rid of his chain.

"Promise me that you won't judge me for my past mistakes and promise me that I can have a small piece of your heart. I know I can't fully have you because you are with Candy, but it hasn't been a day that has gone by that I haven't thought about you. I was naive and stupid, but I learned the game fast. I can't do nothing with your mama, she's in a relationship with my twin sister who's in prison and she thinks I don't know, but I heard your daddy say my sister name when they got to arguing yesterday. Why do you think I've been spending time on this couch instead of in that room." A tear fell from Kira's eye., Drop felt sorry for Kira and he felt like some of the shit she went through was his fault.

"I got you baby! I won't let anything happen to you. I mean that!" Kira wiped her face and started smiling.

"Forreal Drop, you really mean that?" Kira felt like she had been saved.

"My word is my bond!" Drop liked Kira and he wanted her to know she could trust him. Kira stood up from the couch and pulled Drop by his shirt. She led him to her room. She pushed Drop onto the bed, pulled down his shorts and gave him another hand job. This time Drop couldn't nut. He needed more.

"Kira, I need to feel your pussy or your mouth!" Drop was blunt about the situation. Kira stopped stroking his dick and looked him in the eyes.

"I wanna go to the doctor and get checked before I have sex with you!" Kira wanted to have sex with Drop just as bad but she knew she had performed a lot of unprotected sexual acts and she didn't want Drop to suffer for her actions. Her remark made Drop's hard dick go soft and crawl back into his stomach.

"That's what's up lil baby! I appreciate you looking out for me. In the morning go be a walk-in at any OBGYN! I'm gonna pay for it!" Drop was glad that Kira just didn't fuck him without being tested. Kira stood up and Drop pulled up his shorts. Drop stood up from the bed and took Kira into his arms. He held her tight.

"I want you to know that you've got a big piece of my heart." Drop kissed Kira on her cheek. Drop left Kira in her room and he went to the den where he started playing the game. Kira laid on her back in the bed looking at the ceiling while she floated away in her own thoughts. Lay Lay bout wanna kill me now that I've let her old bitch eat my pussy, but it wasn't my fault. I didn't know they were lovers. Candy you fucked JB and think that I don't know so bitch you just gonna get what you got coming to you, thought Kira right before she closed her eyes to go to sleep.

****

Sonya drove away from Drop's condo crying from the way her daughter felt about her. Sonya wanted nothing more but for her daughter to love her, but she knew that there was a snowflake in hell chance of that happening. She went by the stash spot and got an eightball of straight drop then she went to Cal Mae's house. All she wanted to do was escape the misery and pain she was feeling. As much as she hated Carl Lee, he was the only person who understood her no matter what her situation was. This is why she drove over his house since she was about to relapse. Sonya got out of the car and started walking towards the front door.

Psssii Psssii

The sound made Sonya jump. When she looked to see where the noise was coming from she saw Carl Lee in his basement window.

"Come around to the side doe!" Carl Lee knew something was wrong with Sonya for her to just pop up at his house. Sonya walked around the side of the house to where Carl Lee was standing in his door. She walked into Carl Lee's room and he closed the door behind her. Sonya sat down on the bed. She saw Carl Lee had his shirt off and he was sweating. What the fuck is he in here doing, thought Sonya as she watched Carl Lee pick up a bottle of water and downed it.

"What's up love? What's wrong?" Carl Lee asked Sonya seeing that she had something clutched in her hand.

"Where is your shoota at?" Sonya asked Carl Lee and he started laughing, as he dropped to the floor and started doing push-ups.

"I don't own one of those!" Sonya looked at Carl Lee like he was crazy. That dope gotta be fie if it got this nigga in here doin push-ups, thought Sonya.

"Boy, stop playing and give me the damn shoota!" Sonya twisted her face up. Carl Lee finished doing his set of push-ups then he got up from the floor.

"Let me see what you got!" Carl Lee held out his hand and Sonya handed him the eightball of dope she had. Carl Lee walked to his room door that was connected to the kitchen.

"Come here, Leroy!" Carl Lee screamed into the kitchen where Cal Mae was holding her famous Tunk game at. Carl Lee left his door open then he sat beside Sonya. Seconds later, Leroy came in and shut the door behind hisself.

"What's up nephew?" Leroy knew Carl Lee had what he'd asked him about earlier that day.

"Give me two hundred!" Carl Lee handed Leroy the eightball he'd gotten from Sonya.

"What the fuck you doin?" Sonya jumped mad. Leroy hurried up and gave Carl Lee two hundred dollars after he looked at the dope. This that drop, thought Leroy.

"Preciate that, nephew!" Leroy left out of the room. Sonya was mad as hell.

"Baby girl, I don't smoke anymore and I'm not bout to let you start back. Not on my watch anyways!" Sonya wasn't trying to hear the bullshit Carl Lee was talking about.

"Bitch, stop lying, yo crackhead ass ain't been to nobody's rehab so I know you still smokin!" Sonya spat at Carl Lee.

"Ha, ha, ha! Bitch, first off, watch yo muthafuckin mouf and second off, I don't need no fuckin rehab to quit ah muthafuckin thang!" Carl Lee got up and walked to his closet. He grabbed a shoebox then went and sat back next to Sonya. Carl Lee opened the shoe box and Sonya couldn't believe how much money was inside it.

"Nah, don't look stupid now! I been clean almost a month and I've stacked bout twelve bands. I'm through with that shit. It's time for us to get right baby!" Sonya listened to Carl Lee but this was the first time in a long time that she seen the truth being spoken through his eyes.

"I know you thought you was gonna fly yo ass over and we get high together, but nooo. Muthafucka it's a new day and a new Carl Lee. I get tired of not being able to see my grandbaby cause his mama don't want him around no crackhead. Hell, can you blame her? I don't want Bud Bud to know shit about no muthafuckin dope either!" Carl Lee started tearing up. Sonya was speechless.

"Look at all the shit we put our got damn kids through! Hell, it's a blessing they ain't killed our muthafuckin asses. God knows my heart and I'm trying to do better so I advise you to find God and get your shit together too!" Carl Lee cried while he talked. Sonya knew Carl Lee was speaking the truth as she watched a grown man cry like a baby.

"Scarface said you've never seen a man cry till you seen a man die. That's why I'm crying baby. Cause all that old shit dead wit me!"

"I'm sorry baby! I love you! My fault for even thinking I could play you like that!" Sonya hugged Carl Lee and started crying with him.

****

Sweets and Thomas ate dinner at Connor's on Bridge Street. After dinner they decided to go to Bar Louie's to have a few drinks while they listened to some mellow music. when they got inside the bar, they found a table and sat down. Thomas waved over a waiter and ordered a bottle of Hennessy. Sweets thought Thomas was handsome, but she couldn't feel him because his story wasn't adding up to her. She had caught him in a lie about his baby mama which he didn't know that Sweets knew the girl at Chucky cheese whose daughter was having the birthday party. The woman's real baby daddy was at Chucky Cheese. A red flag went up inside of Sweets head at dinner but she didn't want to end the night without finding more out about Thomas. Sweets scooted closer to Thomas while he poured their drinks.

"So when do you get back on the road?" Sweets asked Thomas as he handed her a glass of liquor.

"The road!" What do you mean?" Thomas was confused.

"You know, the highway! You do drive trucks don't you?" Red flag again. This nigga done forgot that he told me he drives trucks, Sweets said to herself.

"Oh yeah, um! I gotta leave out tomorrow!" Thomas took a sip of his Cognac. Sweets looked at his ring finger and saw the indentation of a ring. He said he's not married but there's an indention where the wedding band goes, thought Sweets.

"Have you ever been married ?" She asked him.

"No, I haven't ever been married!" Fuckin liar, thought Sweets and she stood up from the table.

"Could you take me to my car?" Sweets asked with an attitude. Thomas was taken by surprise by Sweets request.

"Oh, um, sure!" Thomas got up from the table to follow Sweets who was almost out the door.

"Hi Jeffery! What's up buddy? I thought that was you!" Said the police officer that was standing outside the bar with the security. Sweets turned around and caught Thomas signaling the officer to shut up.

"Nah, you've got the wrong dude!" Thomas knew he was caught.

"Oh my bad buddy!" Said the officer catching on to what Thomas was saying.

Sweets and Thomas rode in complete silence while Thomas drove to Popeyes on University Drive where Sweets car was at. As soon as Thomas pulled beside Sweets car, she reached for the door handle and opened her door.

"Hold on!" Thomas grabbed Sweets arm.

"Get your fuckin hands off of me!" Sweets tried to move Thomas's hand but he had a firm grip.

"Please just hear me out, Shecera!" Pleaded Thomas. When Sweets heard Thomas call her by her real name that she had not told him, she stopped trying to snatch away and looked Thomas in his eyes.

"Who are you?" She asked him. Thomas sighed and shook his head.

"Close the door and I'll tell you." Sweets put her leg back into the car and closed the door.

"My name is Jeffery Chapman and I'm not from Decatur." He had Sweets undivided attention. "I'm an FBI Agent!" Thomas watched Sweets whole persona change.

"What do you want with me?" Sweets was confused.

"I could get fired for what I'm about to tell you, but fuck it. I can't stand this prejudice ass law enforcement bullshit anyways. There's an investigation going on on your brother!"

"Fuck!" Sweets put her head in her hands.

"It started when a guy by the name of Carl Lee Ballin on facebook posted pictures in an old school car that was worth a hundred grand easily. Then he posted pics of himself beside a new Suburban that is worth another hundred grand easily." Sweets started slapping herself on the forehead as she thought about how her dumb ass daddy had gotten the feds on Drop's trail.

"But once we started watching Car Lee Ballin, we quickly found out that he was a smoker and Ivan A.K.A Drop, was the dealer. Shecara the only reason I'm telling you this is because I don't want you to lose your brother for a very long time. Please tell your brother to shut down now and move out of town for at least a year." Sweets couldn't believe the shit she was hearing.

"After following you for weeks and reading about your past history in our database files, I became intrigued by you and I wanted to get to know you. If I didn't, I would've never gave you a heads up!" Thomas explained.

"Thanks Thomas or Jeffery or whatever your name is! You still have my number! Call me!" Sweets got out of Thomas's car and got inside of her car. She couldn't wait to tell Drop what was goin on but she wasn't gonna do it over the phone. She kept looking in the rearview mirror to make sure she wasn't being followed. When she pulled in front of Drop's building, she called his phone.

"Yo!" Drop answered while he played 2K on the PS4.

"Open your door!" Drop heard the odd tone in his sister's voice. he paused the game and went and opened the door.

"Why you back so early?" Drop wanted to know.

"Bruh, you gotta leave town for a year!" Sweets said sadly.

"What you talkin bout, sis?"

"The Feds have you under investigation!"

"What!"

"Bruh, the muthafucka I went out with tonight turned out to be a fuckin Fed agent!" Sweets sat down on the couch and fired up a cigarette. Then she told Drop everything she knew. Drop was amused by the things he was hearing from Sweets. The more he listened to Sweets, the clearer that shit started getting to him.

"This explains why them punk ass narcs planted dope in my car, but didn't charge me wit shit!" Drop began rubbing his temple.

"So what you gonna do, Love?" Sweets was worried about her brother. Drop leaned back on the couch.

"Shid sis, I gotta get the fuck from around here. Ain't too much I can do. If they down on me, it won't be long before they get somebody to make a buy from me. I got a lil bread, so I'ma put my shit in storage and go. You can have the crib on Skyline, it's paid for so you won't have shit but a light bill." Drop took a sip of his drink.

"Carl Lee Ballin!" Said Drop. Him and Sweets burst into laughter.

****

Niece leaned on the stage while she shook her ass to Rick Ross's song "Trap Trap Trap." The guy standing behind her was tipping Niece a dollar at a time. The night was slow and dude was really making Niece work hard for that mighty dollar, but she didn't care because she needed to make all the money that she could cause she was saving up for an apartment. She thought when she told her mother that she was pregnant that her mother was gonna be happy and tell her to come back home, but that wasn't the case. Her mama cussed her out for dropping out of school and told her she needs to stay where she's at because ain't no babies coming to her house. So

Niece herself was still living in hotel rooms and still dancing at the Player's Club. As soon as the song ended, Niece left the stage to go freshen up, but she was stopped on her way to the dressing room by the man who was tipping her.

"Excuse me, beautiful!" The man grabbed Niece's arm. Niece turned around to see what he wanted.

"What's up?" Niece had a timid expression on her face, but it softened up when she got a good look at the tall, bald headed brother who stood in front of her.

"Can I get a minute of your time?" He said, flashing his pearly white teeth.

"Of course, handsome! Let me go freshen up and I'll be right back. Niece went to the dressing room and freshened up. When she came back out the dude had a stripper sitting in his lap. So much for getting to know him, thought Niece as she walked to the bar. She sat down at the bar and started counting the singles she had collected so she could cash them in. Ninety-eight dollars! Fuck, that's barely enough to pay for my room, thought Niece as she sat the money on the bar for the bartender to get. Niece turned towards the entrance of the club and she saw Marquita walking in the club with an older looking white man, who appeared to have plenty of money. When Marquita and Niece made eye contact, Marquita walked to Niece and gave her a hug.

"Hey girl!" Niece could tell Marquita was feeling good.

"What's up, boo!" Replied Niece

"This is my friend, Randy! Randy, this is Niece!" Marquita

introduced Randy and Niece to one another.

"Hi sexy! Nice to meet you! Which way is the restroom?" Randy needed to go to treat his nose.

"It's that way! Don't you want me to order you a drink?" Marquita pointed towards the restroom.

"Sure, why not?" Get me a Scotch on the rocks!" Randy went to the restroom. Niece looked at Randy as he walked off. He must be a lawyer or car salesman, Niece said to herself as she observed the way Randy was dressed in a Tommy Hilfiger business suit and expensive looking loafers.

"Girl am I glad to see you! Are you down to make some money?" Marquita needed Niece's help. Earlier she was at the Port of Decatur with Randy on his boathouse and Randy showed Marquita two hundred thousand dollars in a briefcase. He bragged to Marquita about how he was a millionaire lawyer and how that lil bit of money was nothing. That's when Marquita told him that they should go to the strip club and have a drink. She was in hopes that she would find someone to help her rob Randy for the money she saw.

"Hell yeah, girl. It's been slow as pond water in here tonight! So what's up?" Niece was ready to freak for a check. Randy came back to the bar.

"Daddy, this thick young sexy thing only wants five hundred to leave here with us and go have some freaky fun!" Marquita rubbed on Niece's titties.

"Then what are we waiting for? Let's go!" Randy was ready

to get his dick sucked and his ass licked by two black sluts. Niece and Marquita smiled then Niece went to get dressed.

Niece rode to Decatur with Marquita and Randy inside of his new S550 Mercedes Benz. Wow, this is nice, thought Niece as they pulled up to Randy's boathouse. She loved the way the lights on the boat reflected off the water. When they stepped inside the boat Niece couldn't believe how nice it was on the inside. Randy went to the bar and poured everyone a glass of scotch. When he tried to give Niece a glass, she declined his offer and asked for a bottle of water. Randy gave her water and then he went to the bar and pulled out a plate of cocaine. He offered both of the girls some cocaine but they both declined his offer.

How am I gonna get out of here with that briefcase, thought Marquita as she fixed her eyes on the briefcase that was sitting beside the bar. I got it, thought Marquita. Then she walked over to Niece and started kissing her. It wasn't like they hadn't done it before anyways. Randy got turned on by the sight of the girls kissing. He stripped down butt naked and sat on the couch. He was a small, frail man standing five foot six and weighing a hundred forty five pounds. Marquita helped Niece take off her clothes.

"Give him some head while I go piss!" Marquita had Randy and Niece naked plus occupied so she could make her move. Niece got down on her knees and put Randy's dick in her mouth and went to work.

"What are you doing, Red?" Said Randy when he saw Marquita with his briefcase. Marquita didn't say anything. She just pulled out her Mase and started spraying Randy in the face.

"Agghh, shitt! My eyes!" Screamed Randy as he jumped up trying to find something to wipe his burning eyes with.

"Cuh, Cuh, Cuh! I can't breathe!" Yelled Niece as she tried to get up off her knees, but she was knocked down by Randy who was knocking all types of shit over. Marquita grabbed her purse and ran out of the boat to her car, leaving Niece with Randy. Randy saw Marquita had got away with his money so he called the police. Niece didn't know what was goin on until she heard Randy explaining the situation to the operator and giving them a description of Marquita's car.

"I can't fuckin believe this shit! Put your clothes on. The cops are on the way!" Randy told Niece but she was too traumatized by the sight of the blood on her fingers.

"Holy shit! What happened to you?" Randy saw blood on Niece's hand and on the couch.

"I'm pregnant!" Cried Niece as she clutched her stomach and balled up on the couch.

"Oh shit!" Randy picked his phone back up and called the operator again for an ambulance.

"Damn, fuck!" Marquita started crying as soon as she saw the two state Troopers behind her with their lights on. She floored the accelerator on her Honda Accord, but it was no match for the Chargers the State Trooper's were driving. To make the situation even worse, Marquita's gas hand was on the E. She looked at the briefcase sitting on the passenger seat and she started crying harder because she knew she'd never get a chance to spend the money. Marquita thought about the warrants she already had for trafficking opiums and thoughts of suicide entered her brain. "I can't go back to jail," Marquita said to herself then she turned the steering wheel a hard right while she traveled at ninety miles per hour causing her car to do a couple flips on the interstate.

CHAPTER 11

Drop woke up and the first thing he noticed was that Candy wasn't in the bed. He got out of bed and walked to the front of the condo.

"Hey baby!" Candy stopped scrambling eggs and kissed Drop. He was shocked at how normal Candy was acting.

"Hey bay!" Drop hugged Candy.

"I love you, Drop!" Candy started tearing up.

"I love you too!"

"I was so scared!"

"Shid nigga, you had me scared!" Drop laughed. "But it's over wit now bay, plus we gotta move away for a while." Drop knew this was the best time to tell Candy about what was going on.

"What's going on baby? Why do we have to leave?" Candy was curious.

"Fix our plates and I'll tell you everything while we eat." Drop told Candy everything that he knew while they ate breakfast. Candy didn't care that they had to leave Huntsville as long as she was with Drop. After listening to Drop for ten minutes, Candy was ready to pack up and leave right then. She couldn't help herself from falling out laughing when Drop told her about Carl Lee Ballin's Facebook page. Drop was glad to see Candy was full of life but he also kept in mind the Antonio nigga's name she mentioned the night they left the hospital. Candy took the last bite of her pancakes and got up from the table. As soon as she sat in Drop's lap, Kira came through the front door.

"Hey, bitch! Where you been?"

"Nevermind where I been! Somebody done came back to their damn senses." Everybody burst into laughter.

"But nah, I went to the gynecologist this morning to get this pussy checked and everything is on point!" Drop couldn't help but smile.

"Baby, can Kira come with us?" Hell yeah, thought Drop.

"If she wants to." Drop said dryly but Kira knew he was hiding how he really felt.

"Go where with ya'll?" Drop and Candy looked at each other and laughed.

"Hell, we don't even know yet." Said Candy.

"I thought long and hard last night and I came up with an idea that ya'll might like!" Kira gave Drop her undivided attention.

"Since ya'll dance at a club anyways and we're gonna need some income coming in. I thought we should go to where the king of the strip clubs is at!" Said Drop.

"Miami!" Candy and Kira screamed in unison.

"Maybe ya'll can help me get a real plug!"

"We gonna get you a plug and we gonna run that check up!"

Kira was gonna prove her loyalty to Drop as soon as they got to Miami.

"Bitch, we going to KOD!" Candy screamed. Then her and Kira started jumping around like two lil girls. This might not be too bad of a plan after all, thought Drop as he watched the girls jump around.

"I gotta shower!" Candy went to take a shower. Kira went and made sure Candy was in the shower, then she walked back to the front where Drop was at. She walked straight up to Drop as he stood in the den and she grabbed his dick.

"Just don't forget that I belong to you daddy!" Kira looked Drop in the eyes while she spoke to him letting Drop know she was serious.

"Hmm, I won't baby!" Drop felt his dick rocking up in her hand. Kira smiled cause she felt his dick growing in her hand.

"I'm gonna take care of you daddy! I mean that!" With that said, Kira let go of Drop and went to her room. Drop watched her ass jiggle in the leggings she had on as she walked away. Yeah, this gonna be a good move for me, Drop thought to himself.

****

Carl Lee felt bad that he had caused the Feds to get on Drop's trail. He never thought that he would cause something so serious by posting pictures on Facebook. He was glad that Drop wasn't mad at him. If Drop would've been mad at Carl Lee that would have been the push he needed to relapse. But instead of being mad, Drop told Carl Lee that he was glad that shit panned out the way it did. Carl Lee began smiling as he sat on the edge of his bed when he looked back and saw Sonya snoring with all of her clothes on. Then he got up from the bed to get his day started. He had to go to the stash spot to get the remainder of the dope to do what he wanted to do with it. Carl Lee had called Sweets and told her to meet him at the stash spot so he could talk to her. He wanted to try to convince Sweets to give her mother a chance. He knew it was further than a long shot but he still was gonna give it a shot. Carl lee went upstairs, showered, then went back to his room and got dressed.

"Where you goin?" Sonya woke up from her sleep and seen Carl Lee getting dressed.

"Bout to go handle somethin real quick. Why? What's up?" Carl Lee fastened his belt and grabbed his keys.

"Hmm, shit! I'm bout to go home!" Sonya stretched.

"Yeah, go help ya son pack!" That raised Sonya's eyebrows.

"Pack! Pack for what? Where he goin?" Sonya wanted to know.

"He'll tell you everything when you get there!" Carl Lee left out of the house.

Carl Lee pulled into the driveway of the stash spot. Then he got out of the car and went into the house. He went straight to the safe and pulled out the last nine ounces of crack that was inside it. No money was in the safe because Drop never kept his money and drugs at the same spot. Drop put all his money on prepaid debit cards anyway. Carl Lee sat on the couch and looked out the blinds, he saw Narcotic cars pulling into the driveway.

"Fuck!" Carl Lee jumped up from the couch and ran out the back door into the back yard.

"Freeze, get down!" Yelled one of the Narcs, but it was too late. Carl Lee was jumping over the fence and he was now on Pulaski Pike. He ran across Pulaski Pike and went into the next neighborhood with the Narcs chasing behind him.

As soon as Sweets turned off Sparkman Drive onto Skyline Circle, she saw Narcotics and police cars everywhere. Got Damn, thought Sweets when she saw all the cops. There was a car behind her so she had to keep going forward.

"Mommie, mommie, look! Police!" Bud Bud was amazed by all the cars with dancing lights on them.

"I know baby! Sit down before they get you!" Sweets snatched her phone off the charger and called Drop. Her heart pace sped up as she listened to the phone ring.

"Yo yo!" Drop answered the phone.

"They are on Skyline! Drop you gotta leave now!" Drop heard the panic in Sweets voice.

"Who is it?"

"It looks like the State." Sweets and Thomas made eye contact as she rode by. Thomas eyes said he was sorry.

"Sis, sis!" Drop had been calling Sweets name for ten seconds, but she had yet to answer.

"Yeah, yeah bruh. I see a federal agent too!" Carl Lee's car is here, but I don't see him."

"Fuck!" Drop hung up the phone a looked out of his patio window. He didn't see any unfamiliar cars so he knew he had to make a getaway while the opportunity presented itself. Drop went to his room and grabbed all of his prepaid debit cards and all of his jewelry from out of his closet. He ran to the den, grabbed Candy's keys and left out the house. He got inside Candy's car to leave, but Candy and Kira pulled up in the rental car, Candy was driving loaded down with Uhaul packing boxes. Drop rolled down the window and blew the horn to get their attention.

"Come on now! Hurry the fuck up, now!" Drop shouted, then he jumped in the back seat. Candy and Kira knew something was wrong so they quickly grabbed their purses and phones and then got in Candy's car with Candy getting in the driver seat.

"Pull off now Candy and go to I-65 South!" Drop laid down in the back seat when Candy pulled off.

"Baby, what's goin on?"

"They just fucked up Carl Lee at the stash spot!"

Zroooom Zroooom Zroooom

Drop raised up in the back seat when he heard what sounded like trucks speeding by them. He saw that it was the Narcotics driving two Ram 1500 and a Camaro turning into the Condos he lived in.

"That's them that just passed us. Put ya'lls seatbelts on and drive normal bay." Drop told the girls as he laid back down and thought about if Carl Lee was okay.

****

"We lost visual on the suspect!" One of the narcotics that was chasing after Carl Lee said into his radio.

"10-4, Roger that!"

"Please, lord, don't let these muthafuckas open this garbage can!" Carl Lee prayed as he sat inside someone's garbage bend that was on their back porch. He was sweatin like a heevin while he listened to the Narcs walk right by him a few times.

"Fuck it, Donnie! Let's go!" Carl Lee heard one of the Narcs say. He was relieved that they were about to give up on looking for him because it was taking all of his will power not to start vomiting from the smell of the garbage bend. To make matters even worse, he had left his cell phone on the couch at the stash spot, so he didn't have a way to call anybody.

"Mane, I flushed my reefa and my pills when I looked out the screen doe and saw them muthafuckas in the backyard. They gone now! Baby, fie dat joint back up, I gotta settle my nerves!" Carl Lee heard someone say. Evidently, it was the person who lived at the house, so Carl Lee climbed out of the garbage bend.

"What da hell! Carl Lee, is that you?" Peanut was surprised to see Carl Lee climb out of his garbage bend.

"Hell yeah, Nut. It's me mane! Help me out my boy and let me in ya crib." Carl Lee was happy to see that it was one of his old partners from back in the day.

"Peel off dem funky ass clothes and brang yo ass on in here mane. Baby, go grab Carl Lee somethin to wear out of my closet." Peanut was glad to see his old running partna had got away from the bitch ass police.

****

Mr. Mitchell sat inside of his small two bedroom two bathroom beach house which sat on the beach of Gulf Shores, Alabama. He listened to the scanner of Huntsville Police Department on his Iphone. He had been the person in charge of notifying the Feds about Carl Lee Ballin's Facebook page. He was the person in charge of paying Agent Craigs and Wilson to plant the dope in Drop's car. Even though Mr. Mitchell had caused so much turmoil in Drop's life, he is also the person responsible for destroying the surveillance camera at the hotel when Drop shot Fat Rabbit. He also covered Candy's messy ass murder tracks that would've landed her in prison for the rest of her life. Mr. Mitchell was getting old and he wasn't in the best of health, therefore he wanted to make sure Drop could withstand heavy pressure and maneuver in hostile situations because he was about to introduce his grandson to a different level of the game.

Cuhhh Cuhhh Cuhhh

Mr. Mitchell's cough had became worse over the past few months. Two months ago the doctor told him he had less than four months to live. That's when Mr. Mitchell decided it was time to see his grandchildren for the first time and reunite with his daughter after twenty-two years.

22 years earlier…………

Tears ran down John's face as he watched his wife Tonya take her last breath. Lung cancer had gotten the best of her and it declared victory over her life. Earlier in the day the hospice nurse had warned John that Tonya wouldn't make it through the night. He wished their only child was there to say goodbye to her mother, but she wasn't because she was about to have John and Tonya's grandchild in Huntsville at the Huntsville Hospital.

John and Sonya's relationship had gone south when he found out that she wasn't going to school and she was stripping at a club. John and Tonya sent Sonya to Alabama A&M because that's where she said she wanted to go to College at. Sonya got a healthy allowance every week and she had a brand new car. All she had to do was go to school, but Sonya wanted to be in and part of the club scene. When John and Tonya caught wind of Sonya's rebellious actions, they tried to get her to come back to their home in Tuscaloosa, Alabama, but she refused. On the day that John was about to go to Huntsville to find Sonya and make her come home, was the same day that Tonya found out that she had been diagnosed with lung cancer. John knew Sonya was grown and she had her mind made up that she was gonna do what she wanted to do, so he made the decision to stay at home with his wife to spend every second that he could spend with her. John knew Tonya was the only woman in the world who would truly love him for who he really was. She knew everything about John and she loved him for all of his flaws no matter how bad it may be.

"I love you, Tonya!" John shut Tonya's eyelids and kissed her for the last time. They say when you lose a life, you gain a life, thought John as he stood up from Tonya's bedside.

Hurt from losing the love of his life, John decided to drive from his house in Tuscaloosa to the Huntsville Hospital to see his grandchild that was born last night exactly thirty minutes after his wife died. John made it to the hospital around three that evening. He went to the souvenir store and bought Sonya some bears and balloons then he went to her room. When he went into her room, he didn't see anyone, but he heard something inside the bathroom of Sonya's hospital room. John opened the bathroom door to the shock of his life. Sonya was sitting on the toilet in her hospital gown smoking crack off of a crack pipe. Sonya was so high that she thought she was seeing a ghost when she saw her father standing in front of her. A tear ran from John's eye as he stared Karma in the eyes. The same drug that he had flooded throughout many cities and communities was now being used by his only child.

Smack!

"Aihhh! Stop dad!" Sonya yelled when John smacked her, but he was

about to try to slap some sense into her ass.

Smack!

"Aggghhhh!" Sonya yelled to the top of her lungs causing

the nurses who were working the floor she was on to hear her. The nurse ran into her room, but John was so zoned out that he didn't hear or see anything but Sonya.

"Call security!" Said one of the nurses. John started choking Sonya making her fall off the toilet onto the floor. Her stitches burst open and she began bleeding.

"Get your hands off of her!" The security started hitting John with the security clubs.

"Argghh!" Grunted John when he got hit across the back of his head, then he went unconscious and fell on top of Sonya, who was screaming. The security detained John until the police came and took him to jail.

The next day when John got out of jail, he tried to find Sonya, but it was a needle in the haystack search because he knew nothing about the city of Huntsville. Four days later he buried Tonya. John hoped that one day Sonya would get in touch with him, but she never did.

It wasn't until ten years later when John was serving a couple of guys from Huntsville some bricks of cocaine and he asked them if they knew Sonya Mitchell. And for sure enough, they did know her. When they described a tattoo that Sonya had on her neck that read RIP TONYA, John knew it was his daughter. The guys informed John that she was still smoking dope and she was still with her dope head baby daddy who put her on the rocks. John became infuriated when they mentioned Carl Lee's name because he knew Carl Lee was the person who introduced his baby girl to crack. A week later John sent his hitman to Huntsville to find Carl Lee and kill him, but shit didn't go as planned. Carl Lee was a smoka but he was also a street nigga. So when he heard it was a nigga asking around about him, Carl Lee took the initiative to go find the nigga that was looking for him and put a hole in his head. That murder sent Carl Lee to prison for eight years. John kept trying to reach out to Sonya, but she was too far gone smoking crack, so he decided to let her be……..

With less than two months left to live, John refused to let everything he'd hustled so hard for over the years get donated to charity or go to ah muthafucka who was only praying on his death. Therefore he wrote out a will to his only child, his two grandkids and his great grandson Bud Bud. Pleased with the way Drop maneuvered, plus he wasn't a snitch, John decided to leave Drop with his Colombian plug. John's last wish was about to be granted very soon.

CHAPTER 12

Sonya was surprised when she pulled up at the condo and saw all the trucks and cars with red and blue dancing lights on them. Damn, I hope they don't have Drop, thought Sonya as she parked then walked up to the condo to see what was going on.

"Whoever called gave us a fake lead. There's nothing in the house on Skyline or over here." Sonya heard one of the federal agents say.

"Yeah, and we're fucked because we didn't get a search warrant for either spot." Said one of the other agents.

"Fuck. Captain's gonna drill our asses out! Man, lets go!" The agents walked out of Drop's condo and walked right past Sonya as she stood next to a few of the neighbors that were standing in the breezeway. Thank God they didn't find shit at either spot! Where's Drop? Thought Sonya.

Once all the police had left and the neighbors went inside their homes, Sonya went inside the house. Luckily they didn't trash the place too bad, thought Sonya as she looked around. Sonya started cleaning up the mess the agents had made after she tried to call Drop several times and didn't get an answer. Ten minutes into

Sonya cleaning up the house there was a knock at the front door. Sonya went to the door and looked through the peephole. There was a bald headed black man dressed in a business suit and tie standing outside the door, so she opened it.

"Can I help you?" Sonya asked the man who looked like he was a lawyer or something.

"Yes. Are you Ms. Sonya Mitchell?" He asked Sonya.

"Yes, I am!"

"I'm your fathers attorney. Your father has died and he's left something to you. Is there any way you can ride with me to my office to discuss your inheritance?" Sonya suddenly felt bad bout the way she had been so rebellious against her father when she was young and now he had died and she didn't even know it.

"Um, yeah! Sure! I can ride with you. Let me lock this place up." Sonya shook her head in disbelief that her father, whom she had refused to communicate with for twenty-two years had died. Sonya locked the door then she walked behind her father's attorney to the limo where a chauffeur was standing holding the door open for them to get inside. Not once did Sonya think to ask the attorney where his office was at.

****

Sweets pulled up in front of her apartment building, but when she got out of the car a new black Cadillac ESV parked behind her car grabbing Sweets' attention. Two big black dudes dressed in all black with guns inside of holsters got out of the truck. Sweets stared at the dudes, she knew they weren't cops. One of the big dudes walked up to Sweets.

"I need you to come with me. I have orders from my boss to bring you and his great grandchild to him!" Said Bolo, who did odd jobs for Mr. Mitchell.

"You got the wrong person!" Sweets told Bolo with a crazy look on her face. Boss said she was a fiesty one, thought Bolo.

"Shecara Sweets! No I have the right person!" When Bolo said her real name Sweets knew he had the right person.

"Do I have another choice?" Sweets asked sarcastically.

"No!" Bolo smiled.

"Okay. Damn, let me get my baby and you gotta get his car seat for me!" Sweets had an attitude.

"There's no need. He has a brand new Cadillac car seat awaiting him in the truck."

"Well excuse the fuck out of me then!" Sweets got Bud Bud out the back of her car and they got into the truck with Bolo and his friends.

"Mommie, I'm hungry!" Bud Bud told Sweets as she buckled him into his car seat.

"Look. I don't care none about ya'll guns, ya'll gonna stop this truck by McDonalds and get my child a Happy Meal." Sweets said out loud. Bolo and the other two goons burst into laughter.

"Ms. Sweets, your wish is our command! Go by Micky D's before we hit the road!" Bolo told Trey the driver. Get on the road! Where the fuck are we going? Thought Sweets.

****

The doctor released Niece from the Decatur General Hospital and Randy was there to pick her up. She thanked him for not pressing charges on her because she knew that Marquita was in jail for robbery charges. Marquita tried to kill herself by flipping her car while she drove at a speed of ninety mph, but she came out of the crash with only a few scrapes and bruises. Therefore Marquita ended up getting booked in the Morgan County Jail on robbery charges.

"So where do you live?" Randy asked Niece as he drove to Huntsville to take Niece to her car at the Player's Club.

"I'm in a situation right now, so I've been staying at a hotel." Niece shamefully admitted.

"Gosh! I'm sorry to hear that. Maybe I can help you if you willing to help me!" Niece looked at Randy.

"Oh yeah! What do you need me to help you do?" She was curious.

"I'm a lawyer and the other lawyers and judges that I work with are a bunch of married men with boring sex lives. Most of them have sexual fetishes that their wives don't know about and they be wanting someone pretty as you to perform certain sexual acts on them. They will pay me for your services and I will pay you. That way there is no connection between you and them except for what happens on ya'lls date. If you help me, I'll let you live in my townhouse where one of my associates lives, for free. It's a big townhouse in Five Points. There's enough space for the both of you!" Randy often used the same game on all the girls that he tried to get to work for him. He wasn't a lawyer, but more like an undercover pimp.

"When can I move into the townhouse?" Niece was excited to get started. Hell, and I'ma be gettin paid too, thought Niece.

"Today if you want to" Randy reclined his seat further back as he drove up I-65. Then he unzipped his pants. Niece smiled when she saw what he was doing. She leaned over the console and reached into Randy's jeans. She pulled out Randy's already erect pink dick and put it into her mouth.

Slurp Slurp Slurp Slurp

"Ahhh, shit baby. That's it! Suck that big white cock!" Randy loved getting head from black girls.

Guo Guo Guo Guo

Niece started deep throating Randy's dick, putting it all in her mouth. Randy felt his nut about to come.

"Ugggghhhh!" Niece vomited all over Randy from the nasty taste of his nut in her mouth. She raised up from Randy's lap and rolled down her window to spit the remainder of the vomit out the window. She couldn't believe Randy had nutted in her mouth.

"Ha ha ha!" Randy laughed.

"Why did you nut in my mouth?" Niece was mad.

"You might want to get used to that baby, because these people you're gonna be dealing with are gonna pay good money to do what they please to you!" Randy informed Niece. Niece sat back and let Randy's words replay in her head. I guess it's time for me to put on my big girl panties, Niece thought to herself as she stared out the window.

Randy pulled into the Player's Club parking lot and Niece got inside of her car. Then she followed Randy to the townhouse in Five Point, a white-suburban area of Huntsville. Niece entered the house before Randy. It's beautiful, thought Niece as she looked around. Her thoughts were quickly interrupted when she heard a woman's voice coming from the back of the townhouse.

"Daddy, is that you?" Said Jessica as she walked up the hallway.

"Yes baby! Come here! I got somebody I want you to meet!" When Jessica stepped into Niece's view, they were both surprised that they knew each other. When Randy turned his head Jessica made a motion with her hand insinuating for Niece not to let Randy know that they knew each other. Niece quickly caught wind of what jessica was saying and she played the situation off along with Jessica.

"Niece, this is Jessica. Jessica, this is Niece." The girls spoke to each other and shook hands while Randy played with the dog. There was something about Jessica that Niece found to be funny. Jessica had lost a lot of weight since Niece had last seen her a year earlier. Jessica was thick when Niece first met her. Now Jessica was considered to be slim thick. Jessica stood 5'5" and weighed around 130 pounds. She was caramel complexion with a brilliant smile and long curly jet black hair.

"Jessi baby! Show Niece her room while I get my daily dose." Randy left the girls to get acquainted while he went and sat on the couch in the den to break down some cocaine.

"Come on!" Jessica walked Niece upstairs to show her her room. Once they were upstairs in the bedroom out of range from being heard by Randy, Jessica's facial expression went from friendly to extremely serious.

"Niece, you must leave now while you still have the chance. This is not what you want to do with your life!" Niece could tell that there was definitely something seriously wrong by the way Jessica was talking.

"Jessica, what's wrong? You can talk to me!" Jessica looked Niece in her eyes.

"Randy gave me the AIDS virus!" Niece immediately felt sick to her stomach.

"He's gonna make you feel like you have nobody else, but him. He took my car and phone. I sit in this house all day, every day and wait on him to come get me to take me to a hotel to fuck with God knows what type of sick-o that wants you to put on a strap-on and then fuck 'em in their ass." Jessica stopped talking when she heard Randy coming up the stairs. Niece was about to say something but Jessica put her finger up to her lips.

"This is your closet girl! It's big with plenty of space for your clothes and shoes!" Jessica knew that Randy was listening. Randy stepped into the room wiping his nose.

"I see ya'll ladies have gotten acquainted, but I think it's time for you to show Niece how it's really done!" Randy pushed Jessica on her shoulders making her fall onto the bed. Niece looked at Randy like the sick muthafucka he was. He knew she was bleeding from her miscarriage and he still wanted to have sex with her. Niece thought about how she'd sucked his dick twice and now she just found out that he gave Jessica AIDS. Niece felt her blood boiling and all she could do was think about killing Randy as she watched him pull out his dick commanding Jessica to come suck it. Niece looked around the room for any object she could bust Randy's head with, but she didn't see anything so she turned around and walked out of the room. Randy ran and got in front of the staircase.

Where do you think you're going!" Was all Randy managed to say before Niece pushed him with all of her might, sending him flying down the steps.

Doom Dadoom Doom

Jessica jumped up from the bed and ran to the stairs when she heard Randy rolling down the stairs. By the time she made it to the stairs, she saw Niece stepping over Randy, who was on the floor barely moving. When Jessica walked down stairs Niece was already outside getting into her car to leave. That was easy. She really thought Randy gave me AIDS! Look at your punk ass. Thought you were about to move another bitch in here with me, thought Jessica as she kneeled down to help Randy.

"Baby, are you okay?" Randy could hear Jessica but he was in too much pain to respond. It felt like his ribs were broken. What the fuck made her snap like that, thought Randy as he grunted from the pain in his chest.

****

Drop was glad he had managed to leave Huntsville before the cops kicked in his door. He had called Carl Lee's phone repeatedly over the past hours but he still hadn't managed to get an answer, so Drop decided to call Sweets.

"Hello!" Sweets said while she yawned.

"What's up, love?"

"Bruh, tell me why I've been kidnapped by some niggas talking bout they got orders from my grandfather to deliver me and my child to him right now!" Drop wasn't believing shit Sweets had just said.

"Fuck you mean, grandaddy? Bubba Lee ass been dead for twenty years!" Drop laughed.

"Nigga Sonya do got a daddy that we ain't never met. Remember, he tried to get Carl Lee ass whacked but Carl Lee killed my mane!" Sweets explained.

"Awe shit, I forgot that nigga existed. Is you for sure them niggas know what they talkin bout? Mane, fuck that nigga. He ain't never did shit for us. Where my fuckin nephew at?" Drop got mad all of a sudden.

"Boy, chill out. His ass sleep in his Cadillac car seat! I'll call you when we get to where we goin!" Sweets hung up the phone.

Drop got mad at the mentioning of Sonya's dad. Drop felt like the nigga thought he was too good for him and his sister and that's why they had never met him. Truthfully, the only thing he knew about his grandad is what Sonya told him, but that was enough in Drop's eyes to know that the nigga wasn't shit he wanted to be related to.

"Bay, what's wrong with you?" Candy's voice snapped Drop out of his daze.

"Nothin' bay! You straight or you want me to drive?" Drop knew that Candy had been driving over four hours.

"I thought you'd never ask!" Candy got off on the next exit where they got something to eat, used the restrooms and then got back on the road with Drop driving, Candy in the passenger seat and Kira laid across the backseat.

****

After Niece left Randy's townhouse she drove to the hotel that she had been staying at so she could get her clothes that she had left in the room, but since it was after check out time, the man at the desk told Niece that he didn't know what housekeeping did with her belongings. Niece walked out of the hotel with thoughts of suicide on her mind. You might as well kill yourself, Niece thought as she drove away from the hotel. She started crying so hard that she couldn't focus on the road so she pulled into the parking lot of Popeye's on Jordan Lane and University. Niece got out of her car to go use the restroom inside the restaurant, but when she entered the restaurant she was caught off guard when she saw the same tall, black, baldheaded brother that was tipping her at the club last night. He was standing behind the register serving customers with the same pretty smile he wore in the club. Niece could tell by his uniform that he was the manager. They made eye contact but Niece broke it and went to the ladies room. When Niece came out of the restroom, she planned on not looking in his direction, but she didn't have to because he was standing right outside of the ladies room when she came out the door.

"Hi, pretty lady! How are you doing?" The guy smiled, but Niece wasn't up for anymore bullshit from a man. She felt like her world was at an end and it was written all over her face.

"To be honest, I'm not doing so good. So maybe we'll run into each other on a later date." Niece tried to walk around the guy but he stepped back in front of her.

"Beautiful, I see the dried up tears on your face and I want nothing more than to be here for your time of hardship and pain. Are you hungry? I just got off. Let's eat something. It's on me. You know black folks love dem some chicken!" His remarks made Niece shake her head and smirk.

"Okay, you win. Get me three wings mild, fries, red beans and rice with an extra biscuit. Oh yeah and a strawberry fanta to drink!" He smiled at Niece.

"I knew yo thick ass was hungry. Grab a seat while I fix our food." Niece couldn't help herself from laughing. I'm damn sholl hungry as hell, thought Niece as she sat down at a table. I wonder what his name is? He looks like a Marcus, thought Niece as she watched the guy move around on the line as he fixed their food. Moments later he came to the table with their food and he took a seat across from Niece.

"So beautiful, what's your name?" He asked smiling.

"Niece. And yours?" Niece bit into her chicken.

"Mark." Niece stopped chewing and looked up at Mark.

"What, did I say something wrong?" He asked her. Niece shook her head no.

"No, it's just when I was looking at you while you were back there fixing our food, I said to myself that you looked like your name might be Marcus. I hope that this is a sign that this is the end of my bad luck with men, thought Niece as she bit into her food. She and Mark got acquainted while they ate. He convinced Niece into sharing her problems with him. Niece loved how attentive Mark was as he listened to her talk about everything, starting with the moment she started working at the Player's Club. Niece began to tear up when she told Mark about her pregnancy and how her mother told her she wasn't welcomed back at her house anymore. Niece told Mark everything except the shit Jessica had said about Randy having AIDS.

"Would you believe me if I told you that your story sounds comparable to my life five years ago?" Mark sat his hands on top of Niece's hand and stared into her eyes. Damn, he's making me weak, thought Niece while she tried her hardest not to look into Mark's eyes.

"I wouldn't have any other choice, but to believe you!" Mark smiled at Niece's reponse.

"Do you wanna go to my apartment and watch a movie?"

"That's it! Only watch a movie!" Niece made that be known.

"I don't want that bloody pussy!" Mark said laughing and Niece laughed also as she slapped his hands off of her hands.

CHAPTER 13

"Miss Sonya Mitchell, we are here!" Terrell reached over and shook Sonya's leg to wake her up. Sonya opened her eyes and looked around. Sonya realized she was on the beach when she saw sand and water. The chauffeur opened the door and Sonya stepped out of the limo. The truck Sweets was inside of pulled up next to Sonya.

"Awe hell nawl! I know ya'll aint brought me nowhere this bitch is at!" Sweets grew Irate when she saw Sonya.

"Just chill, Miss Sweets! You know I got a job to do so just get your son out the truck and go inside with them so I won't have to pull my gun out !" Bolo told Sweets then he got out the truck and opened up the back door for her. Sweets unbuckled Bud Bud from his car seat then she got out of the truck with him on her hip. Sweets looked at Bolo and he waved his hand motioning for Sweets to stand beside Sonya. The only reason Sweets did as she was told was because she didn't want Bolo and his gang to start pulling out guns around her child. Sweets walked up beside Sonya with her face twisted up. Sonya thought she was supposed to be having a meeting to sign some papers, but now she saw that something different was going on.

"Ladies, follow me!" Terrell walked towards the beach

house. Sonya looked at Bud Bud. It was her first time seeing him in person.

"Fuck you looking at bitch?" Sweets snapped when she saw Sonya looking at Bud bud. Sonya didn't reply, she just turned her head away and followed behind Terrell. When they entered the house through the front door, all they could see was the back of a man as he stood in the patio window looking into the Gulf.

"Mommie, mommie, look at the water!" Bud Bud got excited when he saw all the water.

Cugh Cugh Cugh

John turned around when he heard Bud Bud's voice. Sonya couldn't believe she was in the same room with her father after twenty-two years. There was an odd feeling inside of Sonya's heart as she looked at her frail, gray-headed father, who was walking up to her. She knew immediately that John was sick because of his size.

"Hi, baby girl!" John put his arms around Sonya and they both started crying. After a long hug, they let go of one another. John wiped his face as he stepped back from Sonya. Then he looked at Sweets who was the least bit enthused by him and Sonya's emotional moment.

"Hi granddaughter!" Sweets didn't respond, she just looked at John. "This here beef between you and your mother is all my fault, Shecara. Please don't be mad at your mother. She didn't know any better than what she did." Sweets felt herself tearing up while

John talked.

"How the fuck is this your fault when she the one that put me and my brother through all the bullshit for some fucking dope?" Tears ran from Sweets eyes.

"Mommy don't cry!" Said Bud Bud. Sonya saw the hurt in Sweets' eyes and she heard the hurt in Sweets' voice. This was the first time Sonya saw Sweets cry in over a decade. John reached out and put his hand on Sweets' shoulder.

"Baby, it's my fault because I didn't teach your mother about the other side of life. Your mother grew up with a silver spoon in her mouth. She was sheltered all of her adolescence years. She didn't know anything about the streets. Me and your Grandmother Tonya allowed her to move to Huntsville to go to school without warning her about the hood lifestyle. Therefore, when she fell in love with partying and quit school she became a victim of the streets. Your mother is nothing more than my Karma staring me in the face. I flooded many cities throughout Alabama with dope my whole life and my daughter ended up a fuckin' crackhead!" Cugh! Cugh! Cugh! John started coughing and couldn't stop.

"Come sit down." Terrell walked John to his chair that sat in front of the patio window. Sweets and Sonya knew John was very sick when they watched him wipe his mouth with a handkerchief and blood was on the handkerchief. John stuffed the handkerchief into his pocket and Terrell handed him some hand sanitizer. John sanitized his hands then reached out his arms.

"Come to granddaddy lil man!" Sweets put Bud Bud down

so he could walk to John. "Boy you look just like Tonya!" John sat Bud Bud on his knee then he put his attention back on Sonya and Sweets who were both crying. "I know ya'll have been beefing for years cause Cal Mae told me everything. Sweets, you lucky to have a grandma as gangsta as Cal Mae. I feel like if she forgave me for trying to kill her son, then you can at least forgive your mother by giving her one more chance. Hell, if she fucks up again, cut her ass off forever, but please give her one more chance for me." John rubbed the top of Bud bud's head while he talked to sweets and Sonya. Sweets heart was pierced by John's words. She turned and looked at Sonya. "You only get one mama baby, so love the one you have while you can." John added seeing Sweets had softened up tremendously.

"Baby I swear with all of my heart that I'm sorry and my life won't be right until you are part of it." Sonya said through tears. Sweets fell into Sonya's arms crying, letting go of all the hateful feelings and cluttered up emotions that she had built up inside for Sonya. Sonya cried tears of joy while she held onto Sweets. Thank you lord for blessing me with my child's forgiveness, thought Sonya. John couldn't be any more happier in life as he was right then watching Sweets and Sonya make amends.

"Thanks Bolo! You and your men can leave now. I think I might be able to handle these ladies from here!" Bolo and his men left out of the house. "Terrell, you can leave also." Said John.

"But John!" Terrell protested.

"I said leave, Terrell!" John raised his voice and Terrell

stormed out of the house mad. Sweets and Sonya looked at each other with looks of suspicion on their faces.

"Shecara baby, I need you to call your brother." Sweets called Drop.

"Yeah! What's up?" Drop answered.

"Aye love, we made it!"

"Oh yeah! Where you at?"

"We in Gulf Shores! I got somebody that wanna talk to you."

"Hey baby!" Sonya screamed in the background. Drop was shocked to hear Sonya in the same room with Sweets.

"Mane, what ya'll got goin on? I know that ain't mama I just heard."

"Yeah. That's mama. We put the past behind us! Hold on Drop. Here granddaddy!" Sweets handed John the phone. Granddaddy? This nigga must've gave these heffas some money for dem to stop beefin and sis calling this nigga granddaddy, thought Drop knowing that Sweets wasn't that easy to squash any beef. Mama or not, she didn't give a fuck.

Cugh Cugh Cugh

"What's up, baby boy?" John said into the phone once he stopped coughing. This nigga act like we know each other, thought Drop before he responded.

"Shit! What's up?" Drop was nonchalant. John could tell

that Drop had a dry tone of voice.

"Listen. I know you and I don't know one another and you sound like you're not too enthused to get to know me, but I ain't got long to live and I'm trying to change yo life before I die, so where you at?" Drop smirked at the gangsta shit his grandfather was spittin.

"I'm on my way to Miami!"

"I knew you would be leaving Huntsville. Miami's the best choice you could have made. That's where my people are located. We'll be there tomorrow. That way we can talk face to face." Who does this nigga think he talkin to? Like he just that nigga, thought Drop as he listened to John.

"Yeah, that's what's up! Let me speak to Sweets!" John could tell that Drop thought he was some bullshit so he handed Sweets the phone with a smile on his face.

"What's up bruh?" Said Sweets.

"Mane, who the fuck do dude think he is?"

"Just chill bruh! We'll see you tomorrow!" Sweets hung up the phone.

"Baby girl, book us a first class flight to Miami for tomorrow!" John told Sweets.

Drop's brain was running full speed ahead at 3000 mph, thinking about what this nigga who was playing granddaddy could've possibly done to bring Sonya and Sweets together. Drop looked to his right and he saw a sign that read Miami 400 miles. Then his phone vibrated so he knew it was a message. He opened the message from Sweets.

From sis: Bruh, our granddaddy is official. Like a referee with a whistle. You'll see. We'll be down there tomorrow. I love you, be safe.

Drop smiled at the text. He didn't trust many people, but his sister was one that he never doubted about nothing.

****

After chillin at Peanut's house smokin joint after joint of some mid-grade weed for over six hours, Carl Lee was ready to make a move. So he called Uber to pick him up. On his way home, Carl Lee thought about all the fucked up decisions he had made in life. He wanted to do something different for a change. Carl Lee shut the door to the Uber car and started walking towards the house with his head down. He was so lost in his thoughts that he never saw the women from Cal Mae's church walking up behind him. Sister Nancy suddenly felt the power of God run through her veins and take control of her body. She ran behind Carl Lee and put her hands on his head.

"Sista Nancy, what are you doing to Cal Mae's boy?" Screamed Sista Beatrice causing Cal Mae to come to the front door to see what was going on outside of her house. What the hell is this bitch doin to my child, thought Cal Mae when she saw Carl Lee drop down to his knees with his eyes rolling in his head as Sista Nancy palmed the top of his head. Carl Lee felt an overwhelming feeling come into his body and when he opened his eyes all he could think about was going to church to repent and tell others about how great God was. He got up from his knees and hugged Sista Nancy, who was crying.

"Do the right thing, Carl Lee!" Sista Nancy told him "I'm gonna do my best, Sista Nancy." Carl Lee took the nine ounces of crack that he had stuffed in his pants and threw them into the trash can. Cal Mae damn near lost her mind as she watched Carl Lee throw the dope in the trash can.

"Boy, is you fuckin crazy! Hell, I can buy a damn car with that shit!" Cal Mae came outside running, hollering in her gown, titties hitting her knee caps and climbed in the garbage bin to get the dope out.

"Sista Nancy, get yo ass from over here! I don't know why you call yourself laying hands and shit! Got this stupid muthafucka throwing all this dope in the garbage like we rich!" Cal Mae went the fuck off. The sista's from the church knew Cal Mae would shoot something in a heartbeat, so they hurried and left from her house.

Carl Lee went into the house and walked down to his room. He grabbed all of the old empty liquor bottles he had sitting around as memories of certain nights that he had got it up and threw them in the garbage. Carl Lee took all the posters of Rick James, Tupac, Biggie Smalls and other hip hop pioneers off of the walls in his room. He was cleaning his room from all of the negative gestures. After he was satisfied with his cleaning, Carl Lee got down on his knees and said a prayer, but you know the devil was right beside him. Dear Lord, lead me and guide me to do your work,

Amen! Prayed Carl Lee. When Carl Lee got up from praying, he bumped into the shelf that was on the wall causing magazines and DVDs to fall on the floor. When he bent down to pick them up, he stared at his second weakness. A Buttman magazine and Big Dicks for Thick Chicks DVD was looking Carl Lee directly in the eyes. At least I don't smoke dope anymore, I can look at a lil porn, Carl Lee reasoned with himself. Porn and women was his other addictions besides crack. He wastes no time putting the DVD into the DVD player and grabbed his lotion.

****

Drop started poppin Molly on the way to Miami, so when they made it to Miami at 3 a.m. in the morning, he was wired. He drove to South Beach Boulevard and got a hotel room at the Best Western. While Candy and Kira slept, Drop sat up thinking about all of the events that had been goin on in his life for the past few months. He came to the conclusion that somebody wanted him off of the streets. Drop made up his mind that when he found out who that somebody was, he was gonna make them pay with their life. He thought about the last conversation that he had with his ex-bitch LaToya.

Three months ago.........

"Drop! Drop! Wake up!" LaToya pushed Drop in his chest while he lay asleep in the bed of their apartment in

Ashton Place down South Parkway. Drop jumped up from his sleep thinking that something was seriously wrong due to the way LaToya was waking him up.

"Huh, what's goin on?" Said Drop.

"Who the fuck is these hoes writing your phone talking about they love you and who dis Kamesha bitch talking bout she might be pregnant?" Drop couldn't believe that Toya had went through his phone.

"You done woke me up out my sleep with this bullshit!" Drop got out of the bed and snatched his phone out of Toya's hand.

"Bullshit my ass! Nigga you's the one fuckin these nasty ass hoes!" Toya screamed, but Drop paid her no attention as he put on his shoes so he could leave. After Drop put on his shoes, he grabbed his keys and walked to the front door, but Toya ran and jumped in front of him.

"So you think you just gone leave without telling me shit?" Smack! Toya slapped the shit out of Drop. Drop smirked and shook his head.

"Don't put yo muthafuckin hands on me no more!" Drop was more than mad and Toya saw the killer in his eyes. Drop stepped around Toya and walked out the door.

"Bitch I'ma call the police on you if you leave. I bet the narcotics find out everything I know!" Toya threatened Drop, but little did she know that would be her last remark to Drop. He would've forgiven her about going through his phone and waking him up to some bullshit, but when she threatened Drop with the police, she signed her expiration papers with him. Drop didn't play any police games period with anybody. Even though Drop knew Toya was talking out of emotions, he still wasn't gonna go against his rule. He left Toya that night and went to the room with Kamesha, the bitch who had been trying to fuck up his relationship with Toya just so she could get the dick. He never went back to the apartment where Toya was.

Drop's thoughts were interrupted by the vibration and lights of Candy's phone that was on the table next to him. Who the fuck texting her at six in the morning?, thought Drop when he picked Candy's phone up. Drop had been peeped Candy's code to unlock her phone without her knowing. So he decided to see who it was texting her.

> From Tonio: I get out next week baby. I beat my murder case. I hope you ain't givin my pussy to none of those country Bama ass niggas! Thanks for the money too! I miss you Pooh Bear. Call me when you get this message. Love your husband.

Funky bitch, thought Drop as he erased the message. He was mad as fuck. It took everything in his power for him not to wake Candy up out of her sleep. I got you bitch. You better believe that, Drop said to himself as he opened his sack of Molly and then threw a gram into his mouth and washed it down with some orange juice. Twenty minutes later he was so high that he passed out asleep in the chair he was sitting in.

CHAPTER 14

Carl Lee woke up with a master plan. He was about to take the money he had saved up and buy a building to start up his own church. After searching through the classified section of the Huntsville Times newspaper and on Craiglist, Carl Lee found a few buildings that were for sale around the price of twenty thousand dollars. He only had thirteen grand saved up, but he knew he could call on Drop for the rest. Carl Lee met with the seller of one of the buildings, but the building needed too much work, so he met with the lady who owned the second building.

"Hi, I'm Leigh!" The pretty, fifty-five year old white woman introduced herself. Damn she's beautiful, thought Carl Lee as he shook her hand.

"Nice to meet you, I'm Carl Lee!" Carl Lee knew that Leigh had money because she was driving a new Audi A8 and the diamonds on her fingers screamed out "expensive."

"As you can see, the building sits on three acres of land." Leigh explained as she opened the door to the building.

"Yes I see, I'm beginning to think that I called the wrong number. This building's listed price was for twenty thousand wasn't it?" Leigh laughed, flashing her pearly white teeth.

"Yes silly! You are hilarious! I'm just trying to get rid of it because I don't have any need for it. It belonged to my late husband's brother who died a year ago. I don't know what you plan on doing with this place but you'll have to get rid of all this stuff in here." Leigh flicked on the light switch and Carl Lee damn near fainted. Thank you Jesus, thought Carl Lee, not believing his eyes as he looked at a complete church. From the seats to the altar, from the organ to the pulpit, everything he needed was there in place.

"I take it you like what you see!" Leigh saw that Carl Lee was awestruck by the building.

"I love it!" Replied Carl Lee.

"Well, come on. Let me show you the rest of the place!" Carl Lee followed behind Leigh as she led the way to the back of the building. He was already pleased with the building, now his focus had transferred to Leigh, who was one sexy ass cougar. Her long blonde hair and ocean blue eyes were paralyzing to Carl Lee. Every time Leigh looked at Carl Lee he couldn't help himself from imagining her thin lips being wrapped around his dick.

"This is the office." Leigh opened the door that had Pastor's Office wrote on it and she cut on the lights. The office was already furnished with a leather recliner and a giant cherry wood desk. Leigh bent over to pick up a piece of paper off the floor while she was in front of Carl Lee. The tennis skirt she had on rose up revealing more of her gorgeous tanned legs. Leigh looked back at Carl Lee as she stood up straight and she saw how his eyes were glued on her ass. When she placed her eyes on the bulge in his pants, it made her mouth wet. I want that dick, thought Leigh as she smiled seductively at Carl Lee.

"I, um, um only have ten grand, but I'll have the rest in a few days!" Carl Lee tried to get back on track by pulling the envelope from his back pocket with the ten grand inside and handed it to Leigh. She took the envelope and sat it on the desk behind her.

"From the looks of things you have more than enough!" Leigh's eyes traveled from Carl Lee's eyes to the bulge in his pants, back to his eyes then back to his bulge. Carl Lee smiled.

"Oh yeah! So you think so!"

"I'm about to surely find out!" Leigh stepped closer to Carl Lee and started unbuckling his jeans. Carl Lee watched as Leigh pulled out his dick. Lord forgive me, but I'm bout to slay this bitch, thought Carl Lee as his erection reached its maximum extent.

Guo Guo Guo

Leigh deep throated Carl Lee trying to swallow him whole but his length was nothing like she had ever encountered before, so she found herself gagging which was something she had never experienced. I gotta feel this big black cock inside of me, thought Leigh as she stood up and began taking off her clothes.

"Lay on top of the desk!" She instructed Carl Lee and he did as he was told. Carl Lee got naked and got on top of the desk which was big enough for his whole body to fit on it. Leigh was amazed at the way Carl Lee's dick stood straight up in the air as he laid on his back.

"Get yo ass up here on this dick, bitch!" Carl Lee knew what Leigh wanted to hear. She eagerly climbed on top of Carl Lee. Leigh placed her hands on Carl Lee's chest while she planted her feet on the desk, then she squatted down on the head of Carl Lee's dick.

"Oh God!" Screamed Leigh as she felt her insides being stretched to a new width.

"Fuck that dick!" Carl Lee commanded Leigh as he watched her wetness drench his dick. This bitch gotta be in yoga classes or something the way she riding this dick, thought Carl Lee not believing the way Leigh was riding him like he was the last cowboy.

"Ooh shit Carl!" Leigh purred like a cat as she began bouncing on Carl Lee's dick, trying to make her pussy inherit the full length of his hardness. Carl Lee felt Leigh's pussy start contracting on his dick.

"Ahh, yeahhhh! This some good pussy!" Carl Lee loved the way Leigh worked her vagina muscles.

"Fuck! I'm, I'm!" Leigh raised up off of Carl Lee's dick and squirted cum all over his midsection. Oh shit, this bitch is ah squirter, thought Carl Lee as he watched Leigh's pussy pour. Leigh blew Carl Lee's mind when she squirted cum all over him and he couldn't hold back any longer. He grabbed Leigh by her hair and pulled her down to him inserting his dick inside of her at the same damn time.

"I'm bout to bust!" He told Leigh.

"Unload that cock inside of me, Carl!"

"Ahhhhh!" Carl Lee released everything he had built up inside of him into Leigh sending her into another orgasm.

"Holy shit!" Leigh raised up off Carl Lee and sprayed him with cum again. Damn, I thought this shit only happens on porn videos, thought Carl Lee as he caught his breathe. Leigh laid down on his chest.

"Wheew! I really needed that, Carl!" Leigh admitted.

"Yeah, I gotta admit I needed that too! Girl you awesome!" Carl Lee said laughing.

"So when can I get my next payment?" Leigh was talking about the dick and Carl Lee knew it.

"Whenever you want it. Except for Sundays!"

"That'll work for me!" Leigh was in love. They got dressed and then Leigh gave Carl Lee the deed to the building. They walked outside and she gave him the keys to the building. After Carl Lee locked up the building, he walked Leigh to her car.

"Let's say I call you in a week or so for a payment!" Leigh bit her bottom lip. Carl Lee smiled.

"That'll work for me!" Leigh kissed Carl Lee on his cheek and then got into her car. After she crunk up her car she rolled down her window.

"Carl!" She called out causing Carl Lee to stop walking and turn around.

"So what are you gonna do with this place anyways?" She asked him.

"This is my church now!" Carl Lee pointed to the building.

"So that's why it's any day but Sunday?"

"You better know it!"

"Okay. I got you Reverend Freak Nasty!" Leigh smiled and pulled off, leaving Carl Lee smiling shaking his head.

****

John, Sonya, Sweets, Bud Bud and Terrell all flew into the MIA, Miami International Airport, at one o'clock p.m. Sweets called Drop's phone when they arrived in Miami but she didn't get an answer so she called Candy's phone. Candy told her Drop was sleep and Sweets told Candy not to wake him because she knew he was tired from driving. Candy told Sweets she'd tell him to call her when he wakes up.

John had a limo pick them up from the airport. Sonya and Sweets noticed how Terrell always sat next to John. Sonya caught Terrell looking at her awkward several times. It was something about Terrell that gave Sonya a bad vibe. He was too clean cut for one and he appeared to have his thin eyebrows arched. The other reason was that Terrell stayed whispering into John's ear. Damn Fruitcake, thought Sonya as they rode in the limo. John took the ladies on a shopping spree then they went to Biscayne Street where they checked into the Ritz Carlton. The five star hotel was extravagant. John tried to pay five hundred dollars per room for four rooms, but Sweets and Sonya insisted that he only paid for three rooms because they were gonna stay in the same room. Sonya watched Terrell say something in John's ear while they stood at the front desk of the hotel and she was determined to find out why she wasn't feeling Terrell. When they got onto the elevator to go up to their rooms, Sonya put her brand new Iphone that nobody had the number to on record mode and she dropped it into Terrell's blazer pocket, then she gripped Terrell on the ass. Surprisingly, he didn't flinch.

"Ha ha!" Sweets laughed then pointed to Sonya when Terrell turned around to see who gripped his ass. Sonya flirted with him by blowing him a kiss, but he quickly turned back around. I'm gonna find out your skeelo, fuck boy, thought Sonya as they got off the elevator.

"I don't trust that muthafucka Terrell!" Sonya told Sweets once they were inside their room.

"Me either! He look shiesty! I saw you put your phone on record and drop it into his coat!" Sweets started laughing.

"Got damn right, and I'm goin to get it as soon as I get out of the shower." Sonya threw her bags on the bed.

"I know that's real! That's the brand new Iphone!" Sweets laid Bud Bud down in the bed. The Miami heat had worn him out.

Sonya got in the shower and when she got out she got dressed in a seductive Prada outfit. Next she applied a light layer of MAC makeup to her face. Then she put a few curls in her hair with the hot curlers. When she was finished, Sonya looked into the mirror and stared at one bad bitch.

"I know I'ma be fine for a long time!" Said Sweets when Sonya came into the bedroom looking like she was twenty-one. Sonya smiled.

"I'm bout to go get my phone. I'll be back!" Sonya walked to the room next door. Which one of these rooms did Terrell go in, thought Sonya. Then she knocked on the door that she was standing in front of.

Knock Knock Knock

Sonya sat in the hallway for a whole minute before Terrell barely opened the door.

"Can I come in?" Sonya smiled seductively at Terrell. This nigga sweatin and he got some lip gloss on, thought Sonya as she tried to get a better look at Terrell, but he had the door barely cracked.

"I'm sorry but that won't be possible. But here I think you left this in my coat!" Terrell handed Sonya her phone then he closed the door. Sonya went back to her room.

"Damn! You don't play, do ya!" Joked Sweets when Sonya walked in the room holding her phone.

"That punk muthafuka came to the door sweatin, wearing lip gloss and handed me my phone. I don't trust that pretty muthafuka."

In the room next door, Terrell had just given John a hell of a show before they were interrupted by Sonya knocking at the door. John knew Sonya wouldn't understand if he came out of the closet and told her about his sexual preference. Terrell was tired of being John's little plaything, so he had put a plan in motion because he knew John didn't have long to live. Since Terrell couldn't convince

John to marry him, he had to put together something else that would leave himself financially stable once John died.

"I'm about to shower!" John couldn't stand himself at the very moment as he laid in the bed naked. Hearing Sonya's voice made him realize how sick of an individual he really was.

"Well, baby, I need you to sign these lease papers for my loft in Atlanta. The owner said I need to have them emailed to him by the time his agency closes at five o'clock." Terrell pulled out his laptop and pulled up where he needed John to sign on the computer screen. He gave John the stylus pen to sign on the touch screen. John's mind was so far gone somewhere else that he never thought about reading what he was signing. He just signed it.

"Thank you, baby!" Terrell tried to kiss John but John put up his hand and moved Terrell's face away from him. John got out of the bed and went to the bathroom to shower. Them hoes think they about to get my money when I been fuckin this old sick bastard for ten years, thought Terrell as he forwarded the new Will that he had drawn up that now had John's signature to John's lawyer.

Drop woke up at four that evening, still high from the Molly he'd taken earlier that morning. As soon as he was about to fire up a cigarette, Candy and Kira came through the room door with bags in their hands.

"Hey baby!" Candy sat across Drop's lap still holding onto the bags she came in the room with.

"What's up?" Candy and Kira picked up on his dry tone of voice.

"I got you a few outfits, under clothes and a pair of shoes for you to wear." Candy tried to lighten the mood, but Drop wasn't the least bit impressed. Bitch, the first thing you should've been talking about was this nigga Tonio, but I ain't gonna trip, thought Drop as he raised Candy up off his lap.

"Where my toothbrush and toothpaste?" Drop asked Candy, whose mouth opened and her eyes widened.

"Baby, I forgot!" Drop shook his head. Dumb bitch, he thought as he walked to the bathroom.

"Here, Drop. Everything you need in that bag. I got it since I knew Candy was focused on getting you somethin to wear!" Kira gave Drop the bag containing enough soap, deodorant, toothbrushes and toothpaste for everybody.

"Preciate that!" Drop grabbed the bag from Kira, but the look he gave her made her pussy get wet. Drop went into the bathroom. This bitch is fuckin up more and more, thought Kira as she looked at Candy who had a thank you look on her face not knowing she was earning Kira extra credit points with Drop.

When Drop got out of the shower, he checked his phone and saw that Cal Mae's number was listed as a missed call more than ten times, so he called her phone. He was glad to hear Carl Lee's voice when he answered Cal Mae's phone. Carl Lee told him about everything that happened when he went to the stash spot and then he told him about the building he bought for the church he was about to start. Drop was happy for Carl Lee. When he got off the phone with Carl Lee, he called Sweets who put him on the phone with John.

John told Drop to bring the ladies with him to Caviar of Choice, a caviar restaurant. John told Drop that he needed to be ready for the change in his life. Drop didn't know what John meant by that, but he was eager to see.

Everyone was already seated at the table when Drop, Candy and Kira were walked to the table by the hostess. Kira and Sonya were surprised to see one another. Drop figured the older, frail looking man who stood up when they made it to the table must be his grandfather. Drop walked up to Sweets, hugged her and then he picked up Bud Bud. Then he leaned down and kissed Sonya on her cheek. Kira and Candy sat down at the table and got comfortable.

"Everyone, order whatever you want and enjoy yourselves while me and my grandson go talk in private." Drop put Bud Bud down and then followed John. John walked to another table where a short, older looking Cuban or Colombian guy with two big ass goons in all black, standing on both sides of him from the table.

"Sosa, this is my grandson Ivan!" John introduced Drop to Sosa.

"Pleasure to meet you Ivan!" Sosa extended his hand for Drop to shake it.

"Pleasure's all mine, Mr. Sosa!" Drop shook his hand.

"Please have a seat." Sosa motioned his hand for John and Drop to sit down at his table and they did so. Drop knew money when he saw money and Sosa had a different kind of money.

"From my understanding, this is the first time that you've ever met your grandfather who happens to be a great friend, brother and associate of mines.

"Yes sir. This is our first time meeting." Drop agreed and Sosa smiled.

"I appreciate your manners, but please don't call me "Sir." i feel so old when I hear that." Sosa joked and everyone laughed.

"Okay, I gotcha!" Drop smiled.

"Over the past few weeks, you've ran into some problems with the law, that I bet you're still wondering where they came from." Sosa's statement raised Drop's eyebrows.

"Well, just so you know, me and your grandfather had to make sure you were as solid as the two of us, therefore we had to apply some pressure to you!" Drop turned to his left and looked at John.

"You did good son!" John patted Drop on the shoulder.

"That's why you are here with us now. How ironic it is that you chose my city to run to in your need to escape the Bama." Sosa complemented Drop on his choice of cities to run to in the midst of a heated situation.

"Ivan, I just want you to know that I'm sorry for not being there for you while you were growing up. I know I can't make up for lost time, but I ask for you to please forgive me!" John spoke with sincerity.

"You brought my mom and sister back together, plus I wouldn't be who I am today if it wasn't for the hard life I went through. There are no harsh feelings against you. I forgive you!" Drop stood up and so did John. They hugged one another, then they sat back down.

Cugh Cugh Cugh Cugh

John started coughing uncontrollably. Sosa and Drop stood up from the table and tried to give John some assistance but he kept coughing and blood started spewing from his mouth.

"Somebody call 911!" Drop yelled at the top of his lungs. Terrell came running around the corner with Sonya, Sweets, Bud Bud, Kira and Candy right behind him.

Cugh Cugh Cugh

John coughed one last time and his head collapsed falling onto the table.

"Oh my god! Baby NO!" Yelled Terrell then he sat John upwards and started giving him mouth to mouth. Everyone was shocked.

"Baby, please don't die on me, I love you!" Cried Terrell. Sonya looked at Sweets. Drop looked at Sosa who shrugged his shoulders. Not being able to take anymore of Terrell's bullshit, Drop punched Terrell in his temple so hard that he fell to the floor unconscious. Granddaddy was a freak, thought Sweets. A single tear fell from Sonya's eye as she stared at her father lying lifeless on the table. She knew he was about to die, but she didn't know it would be so soon.

A few hours after John died, Sweets and Sonya packed up their belongings from the hotel and caught a flight back to Huntsville. Sonya had to report to her P.O. and neither Sonya or Sweets wanted to be in Miami any longer. Sosa gave Sweets and Sonya five grand a piece and he paid to have John's body transported to Huntsville.

CHAPTER 15

The cool breeze brushed against Drop's flesh as he stood on the balcony of the hotel room. He inhaled the smoke from the hundred dollar blunt of Moon Rock he was smoking. Drop knew he was ready to take over the streets, but he had to make sure he had a complete gameplan. The one thing he did know for sure was that he wasn't about to play any games with anyone point blank period. That's why he was about to lay down the law to Candy and Kira. Everything that has been goin on in the dark was about to come to the light. I ain't got any room for era, thought Drop as he flicked the blunt he was smoking into the wind. Drop walked into the room where Candy and Kira were at, laying in the same bed looking at something on Snapchat.

"Ya'll put that shit down!" Candy looked up at Drop like he was crazy.

"I got some shit to get off my chest!" A lump formed in Kira's throat as Drop talked.

"Candy, I love you, but I also feel some type of way about Kira!" Candy looked at Kira, then she looked back to Drop.

"Before you get mad, no we haven't fucked or anything, but Kira kept it real wit me by being there for you. Even when you weren't in your right mind and started babbling from the mouth about the love of your life Antonio! Then let's not mention that I read a message in your phone from the nigga saying he loves you and thanks for the money. Through it all Kira stayed true to you and it's something about her loyalty to you that attracts me to her!" Candy was lost for words. She knew she had been caught red-handed.

"So this is what it's gonna be. Either you and Kira can be mine or whichever one of you don't like the idea can get the fuck on about ya business right now!" Drop didn't give ah fuck at the very moment. Candy and Kira watched as Drop took off his pants and boxers. They couldn't believe Drop was standing in front of them butt naked with his dick hangin. Candy was astonished by Drop's comments, request and actions.

That's what I'm talking about Daddy, thought Kira. Then she leaned over and kissed Candy on the lips taking Candy by surprise. What the fuck, thought Candy, but she felt a sensation of pleasure pass though her body. Candy watched as Kira layed on her back and started stripping out of her clothes. The more flesh Kira revealed, the more Candy's hormones reveled….

"Come here Baby?" Kira leaned up and pulled Candy down on top of her, sticking her tongue into Candy's mouth.

"Huuuu!" Candy moaned. Drop walked up to Kira and Candy's face as he stuck his dick to their lips. They both started slobbing on Drop's dick.

"Take them clothes off, Baby!" Drop pulled Candy up so she could take her clothes off while Kira continued to eat his dick like it was digestible. Candy looked Drop in his eyes.

"I love you Daddy!"

"Daddy loves you too! Now go eat bay's pussy!" Candy did as she was told and she put her face in between Kira's thighs. Candy had never ate any pussy, but she knew how she liked her pussy to be eaten. So she parted Kira's pretty pussy lips and began licking on her clit slowly.

"Ahhhh!" Kira moaned loudly while she slapped herself in the face with Drop's hard dick. Kira had always fantasized about fuckin Candy and Drop at the same time so by it becoming a reality, she was already about to have an orgasm. Candy penetrated two fingers inside of Kira's hot creamy pussy while she continued to lick on her clit. Drop walked behind Candy, whose ass was sitting in the air, inviting him inside. He rubbed the head of his dick against Candy's soaking wet pussy, sending electrifying currents through her body which caused her to jump as she sucked on Kira's clit.

"Oooh shhit Daddy!" Cried Candy when Drop inserted his hard-as-steel-dick inside of her. It felt so good to Candy that she had to stop sucking on Kira's pussy. Drop and Kira looked at each other in the eyes. Kira grabbed the top of Candy's head and stuffed Candy's face back into her pussy.

"I love you Daddy!" Kira mouthed smiling.

"Tell me you love me Kira!" Drop said out loud trying to be funny but serious at the same time.

"I love you!"

"Tell Candy you love her!" Drop ordered Kira.

"I love you Candy!" Kira gripped Candy's hair tighter, then Drop pulled Candy's head by her hair in the opposite direction and he drove all of his dick inside of her wet pussy.

"Ahhh, hmmm!" Cried Candy.

"Tell Kira you love her!" He demanded Candy as he pounded away at her insides.

"I I I looooove youuu Kirrrraaa!" Candy screamed as she experienced the orgasam of a lifetime. Drop watched her pussy cream his dick. Then he pulled out of her.

"Ya'll change positions!" I thought he'd never say that, thought Kira, smiling as she switched positions with Candy. Drop stepped back and let the girls get in position. As soon as Candy spread her legs, Kira spread Candy's pussy lips using both hands.

"Ahhh Yesss babyyyy!" Moaned Candy as she put her hand on the back of Kira's head. Drop stepped up behind Kira and spit into her asshole sending chills down Kira's spine. Then he stuck the head of his dick into her boiling hot pussy and began stroking her insides while he played with her wet ass hole with his thumb.

"Uhhmmmmm, yes, daddy!" Moaned Kira. Candy couldn't deny the fact that she was enjoying every minute of her first menage trois as she looked ar Drop fucking Kira from the back.

"Fuck that pussy Daddy!" Candy told Drop and he started pounding Kira's pussy like it was the last piece of pussy on Earth.

"Haaaa, haaa, ahhh, fuck!" Yelled Kira. Then she came. Drop felt her pussy walls tighten on his dick like a pair of vice grips.

"Ahh shit! I'm bout to nut!" Drop pulled out of Kira and the girls got beside each other on all fours with their heads in the air. Drop ejaculated and shot nut on both of their faces.

"Haaa, sshhit!" Drop moaned, getting weak in the knees when Candy started jerking and sucking his dick while Kira sucked on his balls. Drop took the pleasurable pain for as long as he could then he pushed both Candy and Kira away from him. Drop stepped back a few steps. He was tapping out. He couldn't take anymore.

Come on daddy, we gotta give you a shower!" Candy grabbed Kira and they went to the bathroom. After they showered, they got in bed together.

"I want both of ya'll to listen to me good!" Candy and Kira sat up to look at Drop who was laying in between them.

"What's up, Daddy!" They said in sync with one another.

"We are a family now and if either one of ya'll cross me for whatever reason, I swear to you, that will be the end of your life line that God gave you!" The girls knew Drop wasn't playing. They knew Drop was now in connection with the Colombian drug cartel. That's the main reason Candy agreed to be in a relationship with Drop and Kira. She wasn't stupid. With or without her Drop was gonna have his way so why shouldn't she stay by his side and ride the elevator to the top? After all, she did fuck up.

"I'm sorry for my fuck-ups, Daddy, but my loyalty lies solely with you and Kira!" Candy leaned down and kissed Drop on the lips.

"I'm ya'lls and nobody else's Daddy!" Kira kissed Drop.

"Ya'll know when a good girl goes bad that she's gone forever!"

"Yes, Daddy, we know!" Candy and Kira said together, then they both laid their head on Drop's chest and went to sleep.

****

Drop shopped for a suit while he called his lawyer and had him to call the FBI's Supervisor of the Northern District of Alabama to make sure that he wasn't wanted on any charges. It's on now, thought Drop as he gave the cashier a prepaid debit card to pay for the five-thousand dollar suit he was purchasing.

Drop left the mall and went back to the hotel to get dressed. Now all Drop had to do was go meet with Sosa so they could discuss business. He got dressed in an all black Giorgio Armani suit and a pair of all black Salvatore Ferragamo loafers. Candy and Kira were shocked at how good Drop looked in a suit. GQ needed to give him a modeling contract.

Drop left Candy and Kira at the room while he drove Candy's car to Nathaniel's, the restaurant he was meeting Sosa at. He pulled up behind a limo when he arrived at the front door of Nathaniel's. He watched the valet attendant open the door of the limo that was in front of him. Sosa, some other Colombian looking dude and two of Sosa's bodyguards climbed out of the limo. Good! He just got here, thought Drop.

BOOM!

"Arrghhh!" Drop felt his neck snap backwards from the impact of a van hitting his car from the back, causing his car to crash into Sosa's limo. Drop looked in the rear view mirror and saw ten Haitian looking men jump out of the van and start shooting AK 47's.

All Drop could do was drop down in the floorboard of the car. A minute later the gunfire ceased and the tires of the van screeched as the Haitian drove away. Drop rose up from the floorboard. His neck was hurting like hell. When he looked towards the restaurant the sight was profound. Sosa and all of his men were sprawled out on the ground dead. Drop wedged the front end of Candy's car from being attached to the back of Sosa's limo and he drove away from the scene with the front and back bumper of Candy's car dragging on the ground. The whole back end of Candy's car was smashed in.

Drop pulled up in front of the hotel. When he opened the door to get out of the car, he felt an excruciating pain travel from his neck to his lower back.

"Fuck!" Drop screamed as he got out of the car. It seemed like the pain intensified with every step he took. When he reached the room's door, he wiggled the door knob.

"Who is that at the door?" Kira heard the door knob shaking.

"Open the fuckin door!" Drop shouted and Kira ran to open the door.

"What's wrong?" Kira saw Drop was slouched over. Candy ran up to Drop, but he pushed her out of the way and he fell on the bed, landing on his stomach.

"My fuckin neck and back are killing me! They killed Sosa!" Drop groused. Damn, so much for the plug! I guess its back to the basic bullshit, thought Candy. The room phone started ringing.

"Hello!" Candy answered the phone.

"Yes. This is the front desk. I need for you to come move your car now or it will be towed away!" Said the front desk clerk.

"I'm on my way down right now! Drop, where are my keys?" Candy hung up the phone.

"They in the car!" How in the fuck is he gonna just leave my fuckin car in the front of the hotel with the keys inside it, thought Candy as she left out the room to go move her car.

"Oh, my God!" Candy started crying when she saw her car. How could he fuck my car up like this? Thought Candy to herself as she looked at her car which was totaled with dents and bullet holes. She got inside the car to try to move it, but the steering wheel was locked up. Candy was extremely hurt. She had let Drop fuck up the car that her first and probably only - true love had bought her a week before he got locked up. I'm tired of this shit! It seems like I've been dealing wit bullshit every since I started fuckin wit this nigga, thought Candy as she walked back into the hotel.

"Ma'am, you need to move your car or I must have it towed away!" The desk clerk said loudly to Candy who was crying. Candy kept walking, paying the woman no attention. When she walked in the room Kira was helping Drop take off the suit he had on.

"How the fuck you wreck my car like that! It won't even fuckin move!" Candy screamed through tears.

"Hold on, Kira! So you mean to tell me that I almost got fuckin killed and all you're worried about is ah muthafuckin car! Bitch, fuck you! Go kill yourself!" Drop was mad as hell. Kira couldn't believe how petty Candy was acting about her car. She knows if Drop tore up her car, then he's gonna buy her a new car. Oh, I forgot her boo bought her that car, thought Kira, remembering Candy's words.

"Fuck you Drop!" Candy went into the bathroom and slammed the door.

"Kira, Google a neck and back specialist. Find one that is open and takes walk-ins. Then call an Uber to come pick us up!" Kira did as she was told and twelve minutes later Uber was outside the hotel to pick them up.

"Give me that bag with those debit cards and jewelry inside it!" Drop got the Gucci pouch from Kira and got out one of the debit cards. Then he threw the pouch on the bed. Drop and Kira left out the room to get in the Uber to go to the doctor's office that Kira had looked up for Drop's neck.

Candy came out of the bathroom when she heard Kira and Drop leave. She wanted to leave Miami, but she had no transportation and her money was funny at the very moment. Candy's heart skipped a beat when her phone rang and she saw Tonio's name. She had been dodging his calls and she wasn't supposed to be talking to him. Fuck Drop, thought Candy as she answered her phone.

"Hello!" She answered.

"What's wrong, baby?" Tonio had been dealing with Candy since she was twelve. So he knew her like a book.

"Nothin, I'm good! How are you?"

"I can't complain! Hell, they let me out today!" Candy

couldn't believe her ears. She immediately felt bad for abandoning Tonio while he was in the County Jail waiting to go to trial for a murder case. She sent him money all the time, but when she started talking to Drop she had stopped answering the phone for him.

"Stop playin Yo!" Candy called him by his pet name.

"Damn baby, you didn't get my message that I sent you the other night. I wasn't supposed to get out till next week, but my lawyer got me released today! Never mind that shit. I'm out, I'm fucked up, and you all I got!" Candy missed her man. They had been separated for over a year due to him going to jail and her going to school.

"I know baby. I miss you!" Candy looked at the bed as she talked on the phone and she saw Drop's Gucci pouch with a gold chain hanging out of it. Candy walked over to the bed while she listened to Toni talk about how much he missed her too. She picked up the pouch and opened it all the way up. All of Drop's jewelry and the prepaid debit cards that he put his money on was inside the pouch. Bitch ass nigga played me with Kira. He ain't got no connect and he totaled my car. Fuck him, I might as well get this nigga shit and go while the opportunity presents itself, thought Candy as she looked at the back of the prepaid debit cards and saw that all the information she needed to get the money off the cards was written on the back of the cards.

"Baby, I got something for us to get right with! I'm on my way to Charleston right now! I got you!" Candy hung up her call with Tonio and then she called Uber to come get her.

When Drop and Kira made it to the doctor's office, Drop had to pay a five hundred dollar copayment and fill out some papers while he waited for the doctor. The doctor came and he allowed Kira to go to the back with Drop while he got an MRI done on his back. Kira caught the doctor gawking at her several times, but she paid it no mind. After Drop took x-rays, the doctor gave him something for his pain, then told him to come back tomorrow. Drop and Kira took an Uber back to the hotel. When they walked into the room they instantly knew that Candy was gone and she wasn't coming back because everything she had in the room was gone. Drop looked at the bed where he knew he had thrown his Gucci pouch right before he and Kira left to go to the doctor. He got sick in the stomach.

"That bitch stole my money and jewelry!" Drop felt defeated as he sat down on the bed. Candy had hit him for over a hundred grand worth of prepaid debit cards and well over a hundred grand worth of jewelry.

Kira saw a piece of paper lying on top of the nightstand so she walked over to see what was written on it. It was a note from Candy. Kira felt her blood boiling after she read the note. She gave the note to Drop.

Dear Ivan,

When a good girl goes bad
she's gone forever!

HATE, CANDY

Made in the USA
Columbia, SC
18 June 2025

59418669R00122